SON OF THE DEAD

DI SARA RAMSEY
BOOK NINETEEN

M A COMLEY

ACKNOWLEDGMENTS

Special thanks as always go to @studioenp for their superb cover design expertise.

My heartfelt thanks go to my wonderful editor Emmy, and my proofreader Joseph for spotting all the lingering nits.

Thank you also to my amazing ARC Group who help to keep me sane during this process.

To Mary, gone, but never forgotten. I hope you found the peace you were searching for my dear friend. I miss you each and every day.

ALSO BY M A COMLEY

Blind Justice (Novella)

Cruel Justice (Book #1)

Mortal Justice (Novella)

Impeding Justice (Book #2)

Final Justice (Book #3)

Foul Justice (Book #4)

Guaranteed Justice (Book #5)

Ultimate Justice (Book #6)

Virtual Justice (Book #7)

Hostile Justice (Book #8)

Tortured Justice (Book #9)

Rough Justice (Book #10)

Dubious Justice (Book #11)

Calculated Justice (Book #12)

Twisted Justice (Book #13)

Justice at Christmas (Short Story)

Prime Justice (Book #14)

Heroic Justice (Book #15)

Shameful Justice (Book #16)

Immoral Justice (Book #17)

Toxic Justice (Book #18)

Overdue Justice (Book #19)

Unfair Justice (a 10,000 word short story)

Irrational Justice (a 10,000 word short story)

Seeking Justice (a 15,000 word novella)

Caring For Justice (a 24,000 word novella)

Savage Justice (a 17,000 word novella)

Justice at Christmas #2 (a 15,000 word novella)

Gone in Seconds (Justice Again series #1)

Ultimate Dilemma (Justice Again series #2)

Shot of Silence (Justice Again series #3)

Taste of Fury (Justice Again series #4)

Crying Shame (Justice Again series #5)

See No Evil (Justice Again #6)

To Die For (DI Sam Cobbs #1)

To Silence Them (DI Sam Cobbs #2)

To Make Them Pay (DI Sam Cobbs #3)

To Prove Fatal (DI Sam Cobbs #4)

To Condemn Them (DI Sam Cobbs #5)

To Punish Them (DI Sam Cobbs #6)

To Entice Them (DI Sam Cobbs #7)

To Control Them (DI Sam Cobbs #8)

To Endanger Lives (DI Sam Cobbs #9)

Forever Watching You (DI Miranda Carr thriller)

Wrong Place (DI Sally Parker thriller #1)

No Hiding Place (DI Sally Parker thriller #2)

Cold Case (DI Sally Parker thriller#3)

Deadly Encounter (DI Sally Parker thriller #4)

Lost Innocence (DI Sally Parker thriller #5)

Goodbye My Precious Child (DI Sally Parker #6)

The Missing Wife (DI Sally Parker #7)

Truth or Dare (DI Sally Parker #8)

Evil Intent (DI Sara Ramsey #20)

I Know The Truth (A Psychological thriller)

She's Gone (A psychological thriller)

Shattered Lives (A psychological thriller)

Evil In Disguise – a novel based on True events

Deadly Act (Hero series novella)

Torn Apart (Hero series #1)

End Result (Hero series #2)

In Plain Sight (Hero Series #3)

Double Jeopardy (Hero Series #4)

Criminal Actions (Hero Series #5)

Regrets Mean Nothing (Hero series #6)

Prowlers (Di Hero Series #7)

Sole Intention (Intention series #1)

Grave Intention (Intention series #2)

Devious Intention (Intention #3)

Cozy mysteries

Murder at the Wedding

Murder at the Hotel

Murder by the Sea

Death on the Coast

Death By Association

Merry Widow (A Lorne Simpkins short story)

It's A Dog's Life (A Lorne Simpkins short story)

A Time To Heal (A Sweet Romance)

A Time For Change (A Sweet Romance)

High Spirits

The Temptation series (Romantic Suspense/New Adult Novellas)

PROLOGUE

*T*he bell tinkled, and Paul Hanson rolled his eyes. His mother was summoning him for the umpteenth time that day.

What the actual shit? She's running me ragged, up and down this damn bungalow all day long, and does she appreciate it? Does she fuck! What frigging life do I have? I've been her carer for the last five years now, not had a damn holiday in all that time. People tell me they know what I must be going through, except they don't. No one, not unless they've been a full-time carer on call for twenty-four hours a day, seven days a week, fifty-two weeks a year, has any bloody idea what it's like to be in my shoes. Why do I do it? Because I love the damn woman, that's why. In the past, she's always been there. When she was fit enough to lend a hand in troubled times, she was the first to step up to the plate.

I owe her. Many a time she's saved me from myself, uttered the right words to prevent me from ending it all. I owe her... big time.

After giving himself a good talking-to, he donned his usual loving smile, sucked in a steadying breath and breezed into her bedroom. "Hi, Mum, did you want something?"

"You haven't fed or watered me in hours." His mother slammed her clenched fist onto the bed beside her.

"Haven't I?" He glanced at his watch. It was almost five. Lunch had been a pasta bake at midday, so yes, time was swiftly approaching teatime.

"What were you doing? Playing on that damn machine of yours, no doubt, when you should be up here, looking after me, or at least keeping me company."

"I wasn't actually." He felt the pimple swell up on his tongue the second the lie left his lips. "I was sifting through the quotes I've gathered for the house insurance that's due next week."

"I told you to sort that out last month. You always need to have those things in place well in advance, just in case anything unforeseen happens."

"Yes, Mum. I remember you telling me. But things mount up, get on top of me, and I lose my concentration at times. You know how it is."

"I do. You're useless, just like your father was. The only two things he was useful for were getting me up the duff with you and using his right arm to down numerous pints at the pub every night," she stated, not an ounce of humour detected in her tone.

"Thanks, and there was me thinking that you loved me."

"Get over yourself."

"Anyway, what do you want to eat?"

"What have we got?"

In his mind, he ran through the contents of the near-empty fridge and raised a finger. "Ah, yes, leftovers from yesterday's roast dinner. How does a beef sandwich sound to you?"

"Dry and disgusting, but then, if that is all that's on offer, I suppose it'll have to do."

Through gritted teeth, his smile still fixed in place, he

nodded and said, "Good. What about a nice cup of tea to go with it?"

"Why ask when you know I always say yes?"

"Right you are then, I'll be back soon."

She picked up her Kindle and started to read her book once more.

Paul marched down the hallway to the kitchen in the centre of the bungalow and got to work. Ten minutes later, he delivered her beef and mustard sandwich on malted brown bread, which he'd carefully cut the crusts off. Accompanied by a mug of tea with a splash of milk and one sugar.

He entered the room.

She took her time to set her Kindle aside. "I need to get to the end of my sentence, I can't possibly leave it where it was. This looks nice, dear, thank you."

"Anything for you, Mother dearest."

She hitched up an eyebrow and gave him one of her looks, clearly aware his tone was laced with sarcasm. "I raised you better than that."

"What have I said now?"

Taking her first nibble out of the sandwich, she stared at him and shook her head. She was never one for talking with her mouth full. "Why do all your sandwiches taste the same, no matter what the filling is?"

He tutted and left the room, not really in the mood for one of her lectures on his culinary skills, or lack of them. Going back into the lounge, he began a new game on his Xbox and was soon lost in his own little world once more. She could go to hell for all he cared.

Half an hour later and in need of the toilet, he paused his game and nipped to the loo. Being the doting son that he was, he popped his head into his mother's room. The sandwich lay half eaten, sitting on the plate on her chest, and the drink remained untouched. Her eyes were closed.

"Mum, didn't you want it?"

She opened her eyes, and he could see the panic within. She tried to speak, but no words came out. Her hand clutched her chest and then fell to her side once more.

"Mum, Mum, what's wrong with you? Tell me!"

He bent low to allow her to whisper in his ear.

"Call… an ambulance. I'm… dying."

Paul sprang into action. Frantically leaving the room, he ran up the hallway to the lounge where his phone was and called nine-nine-nine.

"Hello, Caller, do you want ambulance, police or fire?" the operator asked.

"Ambulance. It's my mother, I think she's dying."

"Let me take down her details. Is she responsive?"

"Yes, but barely."

"Does she have pains in her chest?"

"Yes, yes, that's it."

"Is she talking?"

"Yes, but her speech is a bit slurred. Please hurry. I'm her carer, she's bedridden, has been for years. You have to help me, I don't know what to do to save her."

"Her name?"

"Pauline Hanson."

"Address?"

"Forty-two Whitechapel Road, Eign Hill."

"Her date of birth?"

"Jesus, I can't remember. Wait, yes, it's fifteenth May, nineteen sixty-two."

"Good. Hold the line, Caller, I'm going to arrange for the ambulance to come out to you now. Please be aware that the wait time is up to six hours at present."

"What? You must be joking. Can I take her there myself?"

"If you think you can manage it without causing her too much distress, then please feel free to take her to the hospital. My advice, given her condition, would be to wait. Make her as comfortable as you can, and the paramedics will be with you as soon as possible."

"But she could die, what then?"

"I'm sorry, Caller, there's strike action to contend with today. Either you're prepared to wait or you aren't. I have another call to attend to now. If her condition worsens, call nine-nine-nine again."

"Thanks for nothing." He jabbed his finger to end the call and returned to his mother's bedroom. He ran a soothing hand across his mother's temple. "It's all right, Mum, they're on their way. Hang in there, won't you?"

She turned her head in slow motion to face him and offered up a glimmer of a smile before her eyes flickered shut.

Paul froze. Was she dead? He studied her chest. It rose and fell slowly, and he let out a relieved breath. Then he paced the room for the next few hours, checking her neck periodically, keeping an eye on her pulse. It was getting fainter by the hour.

Come on, damn you, get here fast, otherwise she's going to die!

Another couple of hours passed, and he was alerted by a blue light flashing in the drive. Paul rushed to the front door to open it and urged the paramedics to get a move on.

"Please try to remain calm, sir. We'll need to grab our equipment first," the male told him.

"Hurry up, for God's sake. I'm sure she's dying."

The paramedics, one male, the other female, removed a couple of bags from the side of the ambulance and entered the house.

"Wipe your feet. Mother's got a new carpet in her bedroom."

They did as requested, then he led the way down the hallway to his mother's room. He moved to the bottom of the bed and watched them carry out the necessary tests on her. The female left the room moments later and made a call from the hallway. Paul craned his neck, trying to listen to the conversation, but the male bombarded him with questions about his mother's health.

"How long has she been disabled?"

"For the past five years. I'm her carer."

"Do you have any other help come in?"

"Not much. Funds are low in the community, apparently, and people in my situation have to suffer."

"It must be hard on you at times."

"That's an understatement. Is she going to be all right?"

The female returned a little while later. "We're going to take her in. Can you quickly pack a bag of essentials for her?"

"Oh, right. How long for?" Paul asked, surprised by the announcement.

"A few days. We'll get the trolley in, put her on that and transfer her to the ambulance."

"Is she going to be all right?" he asked for the second time in as many minutes.

"Once we get her to hospital, they'll do their best for her there," the female replied. She left the room again.

Paul removed his mother's overnight bag from the top shelf in the wardrobe and began packing it with underwear and her toiletries, plus a clean nightie or two.

The female returned, and he left the paramedics to lift his mother out of the bed and onto the trolley. She moaned and then convulsed.

"Shit! She's having a seizure. Let's get her in the ambulance quickly and do what we need to do out there," the male shouted.

Panic attacked every nerve ending, and Paul stood there, frozen to the spot, while they whisked his mother away from him. Eventually, once it had dawned on him how critical the situation was, he joined them at the rear of the ambulance. By now they had a contraption on her chest that jolted her body viciously.

"What are you doing? Is she going to be okay? Why won't someone tell me what's going on?"

Minutes later, both the paramedics sat back and heaved out a sigh.

"I'm sorry. We did everything we could, but she's gone," the male said.

"What? She can't be. She was breathing ten minutes ago. How could you allow this to happen? How?"

The male hopped out of the back of the ambulance and slapped a hand on Paul's shoulder. "It was touch and go when we arrived. She took a turn for the worst, and this was the result. We'll take her to the hospital."

"Can I go with her?"

The paramedics looked at each other and frowned.

"Umm… we don't usually allow it, sir."

"You can't stop me, though, can you?"

"Actually, we can," the male corrected him.

Paul shrugged. "I'll follow you in then."

The male mimicked him with a shrug of his own. "That's entirely your prerogative, sir. We'll be on our way."

"What? That's it? You're just brushing me aside? No compassionate speech about you did your best for her? No apology for letting her die?"

"I recollect apologising to you when I broke the news. It's a tragic situation. Now, if you'll excuse us, we'll need to get on."

"What the fuck? You lot, it's just a job to you, isn't it? You don't care about the people you see to. All you want to do is ride around in that contraption every day, weaving in and out of the traffic with your siren going."

"We're not sticking around here to get involved in an

argument with you. If that's your belief, then who am I to try to correct you? Enjoy the rest of your day, sir."

"Are you for bloody real? I've just lost my mother, for fuck's sake—no, correction, you guys have just let my mother die, and you tell me to enjoy the rest of my day?"

"Ian, come on, leave it."

"I won't, Darcie. Who the hell does this guy think he is? We did our best to save his mother, and this is the damn thanks we get for it."

Darcie pushed her partner towards the passenger side of the vehicle. "I'll drive, you're too worked up."

Paul left it there and ran into the house to grab his jacket and shoes and locked the front door. He caught up with the ambulance at the end of the road and followed it all the way back into Hereford, to the hospital. He held back, watching which way they went and was surprised when the route came to a halt at a barrier. He was unable to go any further. His head in a spin, he was confused about what to do next. He dumped his car on double yellow lines outside the Accident and Emergency department and ran inside.

"Hello, sir, how can I help?" the young blonde on reception asked.

"I want to see someone about my mother, she has just arrived by ambulance."

"Ah, I see. Can I have your mother's name?"

"Pauline Hanson."

"I'll try and find out what I can for you, if you'd like to take a seat."

"I'm not going anywhere until I hear some news."

The receptionist gave him a sickly-sweet smile and left her desk. He paced back and forth, his eye on the direction she'd gone in, eager for her to return. She didn't, not for a long time. When she did, she was accompanied by a dark-skinned male. Paul couldn't tell if he was from a warm climate or if he'd recently returned from a fortnight's holiday in the sun.

"Hello, sir. I'm Dr Reynolds. I've had a word with the paramedics who have brought your mother in. I'm sorry for your loss. There's no longer anything we'll be able to do for your mother now. She's been taken to the mortuary."

"What? She can't have been. I want to see her, if only to say a final farewell."

"I'm afraid that won't be allowed, not right now. Maybe you should leave it a few hours and contact the mortuary yourself later."

Paul took a few steps towards the doctor. "And maybe you should mind your own business and stop telling me what I can and can't do around here."

The doctor backed away and glanced over his shoulder at the receptionist who had returned to her desk. He nodded, and she picked up the phone.

"Yes, security. You're needed at A and E, quickly."

"You're kidding me?" Paul asked, dumbstruck. "I have every right to see my mother, you can't stop me."

"We can. Now I have to ask you to leave the area, sir. We're surrounded by very ill patients who can do without the added stress of you kicking up a fuss."

"Kicking up a fuss? Is this how you always treat people who have lost a family member?"

"No, not in the slightest, sir, but your reaction has been very much over the top and is exacerbating the situation."

Paul heaved out a large breath, raised his hands and let them drop to his sides, slapping against his thighs. "Answer me this: how would you be reacting if your mother had just been pronounced dead?"

"A lot calmer than you are right now. Once the soul has left the body there is very little I, or anyone else, can do to save that person. Now, if you'll excuse me, I have other sick patients in need of help."

"You carry on. I hope none of them die whilst on your watch. You make me sick, standing there with that look of disdain on your face. I'm grieving, for Christ's sake."

The doctor reached out a hand to him. "I know, and I'm truly sorry for your loss, but life goes on."

The red mist descended, and Paul launched himself at the doctor, only to find two pairs of hands grasping both his arms before he could reach him.

"Oi, you, oh no you don't. You're coming with us," an older man said. He grabbed Paul's right arm and forced it up his back and, together with the slimmer guard, guided him towards the main entrance. "Where are you parked?"

Paul pointed at his Honda parked illegally in front of them.

"Keen on breaking the rules, aren't ya? I'm going to be giving you a fine for that offence."

"Whatever. I won't be paying it, so screw you, mate."

"I ain't your mate, got that, knobhead? What's your problem anyway?"

"I've just lost my mother, what's yours?"

"Dealing with fuckers like you, day in and day out. Your sort get on my tits."

The two men shoved him towards his car.

"I'm willing to let you off this time. Don't come back here again causing problems, you hear me? We won't be so nice next time, understand?"

Paul opened his car door and gave them the finger, then jumped in and locked the doors. The two bruisers shook their heads and laughed at his juvenile behaviour. It was all he could come up with on the spur of the moment. He started the car and drove off, taking the long way home while he contemplated what lay ahead of him. He had a funeral to organise, but that shouldn't take long. It wasn't like his mother had dozens of friends and family members to inform.

His thoughts turned sinister once more on the final leg of his journey as a plan developed in his mind. A plan that could ruin a lot of lives. Why should he be the only one to suffer?

CHAPTER 1

*S*ara sat at her desk, flicking through her mind-numbing chores before she truly knuckled down to start her day.

Her partner, Carla, stuck her head around the door. "Want a coffee to help you through your ordeal?"

"It's never-ending today. Yes, please, I wouldn't mind. I'm going to ring Lorraine, see if she's got an update on that last case for us. I'd like to get all the paperwork tied up by the end of the day, if at all possible."

"Good idea. Anything is better than answering tiresome emails, right? I'll get you an extra-strong coffee, how does that sound?"

"Wonderful to my ears, thanks, Carla."

Her partner left the room.

Sara shifted the pile of letters she'd partially dealt with to the far side of her desk and rang her pathologist friend. "Hi, Lorraine, can you talk?"

"If you make it quick."

"Oops, have I caught you at a bad moment? You sound harassed."

"I am. What do you want, Sara?"

"Umm… the last case, the Cooper case, any chance you can get the PM results to me by the end of the day, or am I pushing my luck?"

"I'd say you're definitely doing that, but then, what's new?"

"Ouch, sorry if I'm always being a pain in the rear, it's just that DCI Price is going on holiday at the end of the month, and she wants everything tied up in a pretty bow before she goes."

"We all have our crosses to bear, don't we?"

Sara cringed at Lorraine's sharp tone. "Sorry to trouble you. I'll leave you to it."

"No, don't go. I'm the one who should be apologising, not you. It's been one of those days, and it has only just begun."

"Anything I can help you with? You know you can ring me anytime, if you need a hand with something."

"It's okay. I'll plod on. Too many PMs coming out of my ears at the moment. Some straightforward, others not so, such as the one I'm staring at right now."

"Care to share?"

"No, I'd rather crack on and get it over with, if it's all the same to you."

"Of course. Give me a bell if you need me, promise me?"

"I will. Thanks for always being there for me, Sara."

"That's what friends are for, love. Take care, don't over-stretch that beautiful mind of yours."

Lorraine laughed. "Flattery will get you everywhere. You'll have your report by the end of the day, might not be at the end of your day, but it will definitely be by the end of mine."

"If that's the way it has to be then that's fine by me. I'm sure I'll be able to dodge the chief until I have the report in my hand. Take care, ring me if you need me, okay?"

"Yes, Mum. I'll be sure to do that."

Sara ended the call as Carla entered the room.

"Any luck?" Carla asked.

"Not really. I should have the report by the end of the day. Poor Lorraine sounds stressed to the max. Wish I could help her out down there. I know she's understaffed right now."

"Aren't we all?"

"Yeah, there is that."

"Do you need a hand with that lot?"

"Don't tell me you're all sat around twiddling your thumbs out there? You know that's dangerous territory to admit to."

"Umm… just me."

"Grab a coffee and take a seat. It wouldn't harm you to sit in on this for a change. The more you learn about this side of the job the more likely you're going to want to swerve any ideas of going for a promotion further down the line."

"I'll get a coffee, looks like I'll be needing it."

Carla left the office and returned a few minutes later with a steaming hot mug of coffee in one hand and her notebook and pen in the other.

"That's what I like to see, an eager beaver at work."

Carla tutted and closed her eyes. "You can't say that word these days without a certain connotation coming to mind."

Sara's cheeks heated up. "Oh my, I never even thought about that. Forget I said anything."

"Already forgotten. On the other hand, I do enjoy watching you squirm when you've messed up."

The landline rang, interrupting the conversation.

"DI Sara Ramsey, how can I help?"

"Ma'am, it's Jeff on reception."

"Yes, Jeff, what's up?"

"Umm… a pretty nasty incident has just been reported, and I wondered if you wouldn't mind attending the scene."

Sara grinned at Carla. "We'd be honoured. Give me the details, and my partner will jot them down."

"It's twelve Moffett Street out in Belmont, do you know it?"

"Moffett Street in Belmont, number twelve, do you know where it is, Carla?"

"Roughly. It should take us ten to fifteen minutes to get there if we use the siren. Ask Jeff if it's one of the executive new-builds in that area."

"I heard, and yes, it is," Jeff replied.

"Okay, what else do we know, Jeff?"

"The resident was knocked down by a car."

"Hit-and-run?" Sara asked, a frown pulling at her temple.

"Not as far as I can tell. It would appear that the man was intentionally mown down by the car. The driver made a hasty exit."

"Interesting. I take it there was a witness to the event?"

"Yes, the victim's neighbour saw everything, even the driver."

Sara had heard enough for her interest to be piqued. She rose to her feet and hooked one arm into her jacket and then switched the phone into her other hand while she slipped her arm into the other sleeve. "We're on our way. See you in a few minutes. You can let me know if there's anything else we should know then."

"Very well, ma'am."

Sara ended the call, switched off her computer screen, then gathered all the paperwork in front of her and slotted it into her in-tray. "Best place for it, either that or the bin."

"If you say so. I guess I'll never know."

"Believe me, it's no great loss, any busy DI will back me up on that front. Come on, let's get on the road, see what we've got on our hands. This is your fault."

"What is?" Carla bit back.

"You, coming in here, tempting fate, insinuating the rest of the team were all sat around twiddling their thumbs, waiting for some action."

"Okay, you win, this round."

* * *

THEY ARRIVED at the new estate which consisted of only six properties, all individual, huge, executive-looking homes.

"Blimey, how did I not know these houses were out here? They're amazing. I bet they cost well over a million each," Sara said.

"Actually, the prices vary between eight hundred thousand and one-point-two million."

"That's sickening. How do you know?"

Carla faced her and grinned. "I keep my ear to the ground."

"Fair enough. I'm not even going to ask what type of people can afford to buy one."

"The usual, doctors, solicitors, barristers."

Sara parked the car close to the cordon and flashed her ID at the officer manning the tape. "DI Sara Ramsey. Has the pathologist been informed yet?"

The young uniformed officer nodded. "Yes, ma'am, she and her team are on their way."

"Good. We'll get our protective gear on, take a look at the scene, and then go from there. Were you the first to arrive?"

"Yes, ma'am. Me and my partner. She's over there, speaking to the neighbours, trying to calm them down."

"Who found the body?"

He thumbed over his shoulder at a woman in her thirties. "Lady over there. She lives right next door to the victim. Saw everything, she did, that's why she's so distraught."

"Okay. We'll take a look and then have a wee chat with her."

"Very well, ma'am."

Sara and Carla went back to the car and removed two new protective paper suits and finished their ensemble off with blue shoe covers that they added once they were beyond the cordon and within a foot of the crime scene. They walked over to the victim and assessed his injuries without touching the body. One of his legs was bent awkwardly, obviously broken. He was lying facedown on the tarmac, his head resting on one of his arms. The other was outstretched.

"Had he been seeking help? Was he still alive once he got struck?" Sara asked.

"So it would seem to me. Blimey, he must have been in agony."

"Yeah, and some. We'll need to get the lowdown on what occurred after he was struck from the witness, if she's up to it."

They both glanced in the neighbour's direction.

"Good luck with that, she seems too distraught to me."

"Me, too. She shouldn't be out here still, viewing the body. Okay, I've seen enough for now. Let's get her inside, see if we can get any sense out of her."

They stripped off their suits and deposited them in the waiting black bag the officer had placed near the tape.

"Not good, is it, ma'am?" the constable said.

"Not at all. We'll leave it there for now and go and interview the witness."

They walked towards the woman who was being comforted by the female officer who seemed uncomfortable to be there.

Sara and Carla both showed their warrant cards.

"I'm sorry you had to witness the incident, Mrs...?"

Sniffling, she replied, "So am I, believe me. That image is going to haunt my days and nights for years to come. Poor Hugh. All he was doing was getting into his car. I think he'd left something in the house. He'd just pulled off the drive and was doubling back on foot. I'm Lucy Childs, by the way."

"Did he appear to be stressed, Mrs Childs?"

"Yes, no. I mean, I couldn't really tell." A shaking hand swept back a stray blonde hair from her face. Her mascara had run, and her foundation had streaky patches here and there.

"Why don't we go inside? Being out here isn't doing you any good at all."

"Yes, okay, you're right. I can't keep staring at him twenty-four hours a day, it's not going to do much good, is it? He was a good friend, he and his wife, Anne. I've rung her but I couldn't get hold of her. I think she must be in court or something."

"She's a solicitor?"

"Yes."

"And the victim?"

"He was a doctor, a GP at a surgery in town at the new medical centre which opened a few years ago."

"Down by the railway station, is that the one?" Sara asked.

"Yes. That's right. Come in, I could do with a drink." She cast another glance over her shoulder at the victim and shook her head. "Poor man. He didn't deserve this. Not someone as caring in the community as he was. One of the best doctors in the area, apparently."

She led the way to the house next door to the victim's. It was a mock-Tudor design with a grand oak porch off a sweeping drive. The planting was exceptional, obviously landscaped by a professional and probably kept in tiptop condition by a regular gardener. She pushed open the large oak front door and revealed an entrance hall that took Sara's breath away. There were feature oak beams the length and breadth of it, on the ceilings and in the walls. Everywhere else had been painted white, enhancing the colour of the wood.

"You have a truly beautiful home," Sara couldn't resist telling the woman.

"Thanks, that's kind of you to say. Come through to the kitchen. Do you want a drink?"

"A coffee would be lovely. What about our shoes?"

"You're fine. It's tiled throughout, and it's dry out today, so no problem."

"Did you have a hand in the design?"

"Yes, my husband is an architect, and he ensured all the materials were locally sourced. We're doing our best for the environment. It's a Passive House."

"How wonderful, Mrs Childs, especially in the current climate."

"Exactly. Please, call me Lucy."

She opened the double glass doors that led into a low-ceilinged kitchen that had glossy red cabinets. Not the type of units Sara had been expecting, but the effect was stunning all the same. The back wall consisted of bi-fold glass doors that again led on to a beautifully manicured garden. A large pergola tunnel dominated the centre of the lawn. Sara could only imagine what the garden must look like throughout the summer months.

Rather than say how amazing the woman's house was again, she asked, "Do you want me to make the drinks?"

Lucy waved a hand. "My equipment is pretty complex. I'm afraid you'd be lost using it, no offence."

"None taken. Two coffees, white with one sugar then, please."

"Take a seat at the table, I won't be long."

Sara and Carla sat at the large round oak table, and Sara

watched Lucy put filter coffee into a machine. Seconds later the steam emerged. Then she poured milk into a metal jug and put it under a chrome nozzle. The noise was horrendous but only lasted seconds. Lucy then poured the coffee into three cups and added the frothy milk on top. She carried the cups and saucers to the table on a silver tray and placed a bowl of sugar lumps in between them.

"Please, help yourselves."

Sara was the first to reach for the tiny tongs and put two cubes of demerara sugar in her cup, then slid the bowl in Carla's direction. After stirring her drink and taking a sip, she asked, "Maybe you can tell us what you witnessed today?"

Carla flipped open her pad and then plopped two lumps of sugar into her cup. Her partner didn't get a chance to take a sip of her drink because Lucy started speaking.

"The car came screeching around the corner. Hugh and I both stared at each other. I screamed for Hugh to get out of the way, but he appeared to be frozen to the spot. The car came hurtling towards him. I saw the driver, he had a vile, evil expression on his face and he deliberately ran him down."

"What happened after he knocked Hugh down? Did he leave the area immediately or did he hang around for a few seconds, possibly to make sure he was dead?"

Sniffling, she replied, "It was dreadful, pure evil what he did. Unbelievably, he reversed over Hugh, then sat there and tipped back his head and laughed. That's another image I will never get rid of in a month of Sundays. How can someone be that wicked, that cold-hearted and despicable? He took pleasure in killing Hugh. I swear, if I hadn't run back inside my house, I reckon he would have come after me as well."

"Thank goodness you weren't frozen to the spot, too. A

lot of people in your position wouldn't have had the fore-thought to leave the scene or get away from danger like that."

Lucy twirled her cup in its saucer and said, "But I feel so bad for letting Hugh down. Maybe he was still alive. I know CPR, perhaps I could have saved him, had I had my wits about me."

"You mustn't think like that. Your survival instinct kicked in when it was needed. If it hadn't, then I dread to think what might have happened to you if you had remained outside," Sara said, doing her best to reassure the woman.

"Thank you. Your kind words can't help me get over the desperation I had running through me as the incident occurred, though. I never want to be put in that situation again. To feel utterly helpless while another person takes a friend's life like that, it's just… well, horrendous." She ended her sentence on a sob.

Sara reached out a hand. "You can't keep punishing yourself like this. It was an incident out of your hands. By what you've told us, you couldn't have done anything to prevent it from happening."

"I guess you're right. Watching someone you regarded as a good friend, their life being extinguished in the most grue-some of ways, is well… soul-destroying, I can tell you."

"I can imagine. Did you leave a message for his wife to ring you?"

"No, I wouldn't have known what to tell her without putting the fear of God into her. I'll keep trying her mobile until I get through."

"Can you give us her number? We'll need to get in touch with her ourselves."

"Oh yes, of course. Maybe you should be the one to inform her. I don't think I could hold it together long enough to tell her. They adored one another."

"Do they have a family?"

"Yes, they have a daughter, Kimberley. She's at Oxford University, studying to be a doctor, like her father." She shook her head and sighed. "My God, that family... mother and daughter will both be in pieces after they hear the news. How awful for them to have to contend with this. It's bad enough to lose someone through illness at Hugh's age, but... to be mown down... murdered in broad daylight, it beggars belief, it really does. I'm so glad my daughter wasn't around to witness it. She'd not long left; she had arranged to meet her friends in town."

"I'm glad she didn't see it as well. Can you describe the car for us?"

"It was dark blue, possibly black, so I might be wrong, but I believe it was a Honda. Sorry, I didn't get the model."

Sara smiled. "You've told us more than enough." She rang the station immediately to issue an alert with the desk sergeant, relaying the information Lucy had given her then hung up. She ended the call with a hopeful feeling surging through her veins. "What about the driver? Was there anything distinctive about him?"

"I don't think so. He bared his teeth at me. They appeared to be in good condition—sorry, I'm a dentist, it's the first thing I notice. He had short brown hair. A slim face. Obviously I can't tell you what height or build he was as he was sitting down at the time."

"That's great. You've given us a fair bit to go on, far more than most witnesses get to furnish us with in such circumstances. How are you feeling now?"

"Very shaken up still. Scared to close my eyes, fearing the images that might emerge. Why him? He was such a caring doctor. He won a national award, you know, one of those caring in the community awards they dish out to people who have gone above and beyond at times. He was always doing that, going above and beyond. He infuriated his wife, often

23

putting his patients' needs before his own. I know they had to cancel a holiday last year because one of his patients was having a rough time in hospital. He's been known to visit his patients after they've had operations. How many doctors do you know who would do that?"

"Not many. Did his caring nature cause friction in his marriage?"

"No, not really, although I suppose it did when they cancelled their holiday. Anne loved him to pieces, they both did. Kimberley is a real daddy's girl. She's never wanted for anything but she's a lovely girl, no airs or graces just because of who her parents are. She thrives to be as good as her father is, I mean was. God, they're going to be devastated when they hear the news, who wouldn't be?"

"They sound a loving family. Until we get the investigation underway, we won't know who the murderer is or what his motive was for killing Hugh. We'll check with the surgery, see if they can shed any light on what might have gone on."

"You think a patient is to blame for this atrocity?" Lucy asked, shocked.

Sara shrugged. "Truthfully, I just can't say right now. It's usually our first port of call during an investigation, to speak with a victim's work colleagues."

"Oh my, I find that incredibly hard to believe. What I'm struggling to get my head around is the fact that the driver was desperate to make sure he was dead, you know, by reversing over him like that. The man must have been crazy, and yes, I mean in the literal sense. Who would do such a thing?"

"That's what we intend to find out. My concern right now lies with you. Do you have anyone who can come and be with you? I don't think you should be alone at this time."

"My best friend, Jane. I'm sure she'll come over. Please,

SON OF THE DEAD

don't worry about me, you should be out there, hunting down the bastard who did this to poor Hugh."

"We will get going soon, I promise. The alert is out for the car. We'll be able to track the vehicle through CCTV footage around the area. He won't get far, I can assure you."

"That's good to know." Just then, her mobile rang, and she left her seat to collect the phone from the island behind her. "Shit, it's Anne. She'll have seen that I've tried to ring her several times. What do I do?"

"Answer it and then pass the phone over to me, I'll handle it."

She sucked in a couple of deep breaths then answered the call. "Anne, hi. Yes, I did. Hang on, I have someone here who needs to speak with you."

Sara gulped down the saliva that had seeped into her mouth. "Hello, Anne. I'm DI Sara Ramsey from the West Mercia Police."

"The police? Why are you at Lucy's house? Wait, she said you wanted to speak with me, why?"

"Where are you?"

"Outside the courtroom in the city centre, why?" she repeated, the panic rising in her voice.

"And your next stop is where?"

"I'm on my way back to the office. You're worrying me now, is there something wrong? Has something happened to a member of my family?"

"Where do you work? I'd like to come over and see you."

"Sounds ominous. Can't you tell me over the phone?"

Sara rolled her eyes. "I'd rather not. What firm are you with, Anne?"

"Blake and Cartwrights in the centre of town, up near the eateries, do you know it?"

Sara nodded. "I do. I'll see you in around twenty minutes."

"Okay." Anne ended the call.

"She's going to be thinking all sorts now," Lucy said. "I know you had a tough choice to make, and it's not the done thing, informing someone of a loved one's passing over the phone, but heck, I dread to think what will be running through her mind now as she makes her way back to the office. Luckily, I know she always walks, never drives to the courthouse."

"That's a blessing. Okay, we're going to have to get going now. Please give your friend, Jane, a call, see if she'll come and sit with you. If nothing else, it'll ease my conscience."

"I'll do it now. Like I said before, please don't worry about me, I should be the least of your worries. God, I wish I could be there, with Annie, when you break the news to her." Tears formed, and she wiped them away with a tissue.

"She'll be fine. We'll stay with her for as long as necessary. Thanks so much for all your help today. Take care of yourself." Sara finished the rest of her delicious coffee, and she and Carla left the house.

Lucy waved them off at the front door and then closed it firmly behind her.

"I hope she's going to be all right," Carla said.

"Me, too. Such a shock, seeing your friend killed outright like that."

CHAPTER 2

*D*uring the trip back into town, Sara ran through the different ways she could share the news to Anne Blake once they arrived at her office.

"I can tell you're stressing out about this. Come on, Sara, you're not going to be telling her something you haven't told hundreds of family members or work colleagues before."

"I suppose you're right. Not sure why I feel differently about this one."

"I do, it's because she's a solicitor and you sense she's going to intimidate you."

Sara shot Carla a dubious look. "I wouldn't necessarily say that's the case, but then, maybe you're right. I don't know, it's not worth worrying about it until we get there and see what her reaction is going to be."

"I can imagine how she's going to react."

"Don't say that. You're supposed to be cheering me on, not making me doubt my every thought."

Carla sniggered. "Sorry, I can be such a bitch at times."

"You said it. Right, we're almost there now. I hope we can find a parking space."

Carla pointed. "I'd slot it in there, it's close enough, we can leg it the rest of the way."

"Get you. I'm not legging it anywhere. I might walk, though, how's that?"

Poking her tongue out at her, Carla added a tut as Sara parked the car. Next, and unsure why she felt the need to do it, Sara ran a comb through her hair before she got out. It proved to be a waste of time when a sudden gust of wind undid all her hard work, amusing Carla into the bargain.

"Damn wind, what's the point?"

"I'm saying nothing. It's this way, as far as I can remember. She should be back in her office by now if she set off on foot at the same time as us."

"We're going to find out soon enough. I don't mind admitting, my nerves are jangling and getting worse instead of better."

"Do you want to stop off and grab a quick drink in the pub over the road?"

"Not particularly, I'd rather keep a clear head, for now. That's subject to change after I've delivered the killer blow."

"My shout."

"Nope, not tempted. Let's get it over with." Sara paused outside the solicitor's office and sucked in a few deep breaths then pushed open the door.

A young woman, early twenties with black shoulder-length hair and wearing multi-coloured spectacles was sitting behind a well-organised reception desk, the obligatory potted palm a few feet behind her, giving the impression they were either down on the south coast in Torquay or at a tropical retreat across the globe.

Sara produced her ID. "Hi, I believe Anne Blake is expecting us. DI Sara Ramsey and DS Carla Jameson."

"Ah, yes. She told me to show you straight through to her

office the moment you get here. I'll just flick the answer-phone on and show you through."

"Thanks."

The receptionist swept past them, and Sara and Carla followed her through a narrow corridor to a large office at the rear of the building. Behind the antique desk, a smartly dressed woman in her mid-to-late fifties sat, peering over dozens of manilla folders.

"Ah, there you are. Can Fiona get either of you a drink?"

"We're fine, thank you," Sara spoke for both herself and Carla.

"Take a seat. Now, I'm intrigued to know what this is all about. Why couldn't you have told me over the phone?"

"It's a delicate subject, one that should be dealt with in person, Mrs Blake."

"Call me Anne. Well, you'd better get on with it. As you can see, I have a glut of work to get through today. Wait, is this to do with a case I'm working on?"

"Umm... no, it's not. It's with regret that we have some bad news for you. Earlier today, your husband was found dead outside your home."

Anne stared at her until the news sank in. Her upright frame visibly crumpled, and her shoulders slumped. Her hands covered her face, and she sobbed. It was an uncomfortable moment or two for Sara to go through, but it was nothing to what Anne Blake was having to contend with.

After several moments of silence had passed, Anne dropped her hands and pulled her shoulders back. "How? How did he die?"

"We're sorry to have to inform you that we believe your husband was intentionally murdered."

"What are you saying? I don't believe what I'm hearing. What proof do you have?"

"Your neighbour, Lucy, saw the incident."

"What?" Anne's brow furrowed, and her gaze darted around the room, landing back on Sara after a while. "Is that why she was trying so hard to contact me? To tell me Hugh was gone?"

"Yes. As you can imagine, she's very distraught that she had to witness such an ordeal."

"Is she all right? Is she still at home? I should call her, see if she's okay. We're very close, our families do all sorts together... What am I saying? Of course she's not all right. I need to get over there." She went to stand, but her legs gave way beneath her.

Sara raised a hand. "Take your time. Lucy is fine, she was going to call a friend to go and sit with her."

"Good, she's such a sensitive soul. Lost her mother to liver cancer at the beginning of the year. As a family, we helped her deal with the consequences. Her mother was an incredibly wealthy woman, and her estate was a very complex matter to deal with."

"Sorry to hear that."

"It's in the past now, we got her through it, together, Hugh and I, and now you're here telling me my husband is gone. I don't know what to say. My mind is shot. How does something like this even happen? How did he die? You said Lucy saw the incident, what incident?"

"Your husband was intentionally mown down by a car, outside your house."

Anne's face crumpled again, and fresh tears trailed down her cheeks as she shook her head. "Excuse me for my weakness, he was my world, my everything. Our world. God, Kimberley, how the hell am I going to tell her that her father is dead? How? It's not something you choose to rehearse in this life, is it? Telling your daughter that she'll never see her father again? Have you caught the person responsible for his *murder?*"

"No, not yet, but I'm sure we'll catch him soon enough. Lucy was able to give us the make and possible model of the car. I immediately issued an alert. We're hopeful something will come of that soon. Our priority is to break the news to the victim's family before we go ahead and begin our investigation in earnest."

"You've done that now, you should go. I want this person caught and punished for destroying my family. What was this maniac's motive, do you know?"

"Sadly, not yet. We won't know that until we find him. You have my word that we're going to do our best to make sure he's caught swiftly."

"Good."

"Maybe you can tell us if your husband had received any kind of threats lately?"

"Threats? He was a doctor, for God's sake, and an exceptional one at that. Why would he receive any form of threat? You think a patient did this to him? I can't believe it. But why? He was one in a million. Always keen to bend over backwards and put in the extra hours if a patient needed him. Why on earth would someone want to kill him? To rob us…? None of this makes any sense to me whatsoever."

"Sorry to have to bombard you with questions at such a horrendous time, but if there is anything you can think of that would help with our investigation. Anything at all?"

"I can't. My mind is blown. All I can think about right now is finding a way of telling my daughter that she's never going to see, or receive a cuddle from her father, ever again. How dare someone sweep into our lives and tear it apart in such a crude way, how dare they?"

Sara nodded. "What about other family members? Have either of you fallen out with any of them lately?"

"No, most of them live down south, we're originally from London. We moved here when Kimberley was seven, almost thirteen years ago. We came here for a better life, a more tranquil, peaceful life, rather than live in the rat race of a London suburb for the rest of our days. We love it here. Hugh was so proud of working at the new medical centre, honoured to be involved with his colleagues there. What am I going to do without him? No, I know you won't be able to answer that. I just can't imagine life without him. He was my soulmate, my constant companion since we were at university together. Our daughter is following in our footsteps, going to Oxford—in her father's footsteps, I should say."

"I appreciate how difficult the next few days or weeks are going to be for you. If there's anything we can do to help, you only have to ask. How will you tell your daughter?"

"I'll need to drive to Oxford and tell her face to face. I wouldn't dream of breaking such grave news over the phone. She's going to be mortified." She shook her head, and her chin dipped to rest on her chest.

"Such a difficult chore, I feel for you. Again, if there's anything we can do to help, all you have to do is ask."

Anne's head rose once more, and she looked Sara in the eye. "What I need you to do is find the bastard who did this. You won't do that sitting here, will you?"

Her heart thumping wildly, Sara admitted, "No, you're right, we won't. However, I can't break this type of news and leave you, not right away. That would be me showing little or no compassion, I'm not like that."

"I'm sorry. I shouldn't take this out on you. Different emotions keep emerging that are, quite frankly, foreign to me. I'm usually such a strong-willed character, nothing ever fazes me, but I have to say I'm struggling to know how to react. I've lost the other part of me. For what? As far as I know, Hugh has never wronged anyone in his life before, so who the hell would want him dead?"

"There is another angle it would be remiss of us not to consider."

Anne inclined her head. "Go on, what's that?"

"That this has something to do with your job as opposed to your husband's role in the community."

Anne gasped. "I hope you're joking, Inspector?"

"Hardly. You're a solicitor, there have to be days when you tick people off. What sort of solicitor are you?"

"A pretty damn good one, if that's what you're asking."

"Sorry, maybe I should have made my question clearer. What field do you specialise in?"

"Ah, yes, I see now. Family law and all that entails."

"Off the top of your head, can you recall anyone who might want to take revenge on you due to a dubious outcome of a case, shall we say?"

Anne stared at her, her eyes screwed up, intimating to Sara that she was lost in thought.

"Possibly. I had one young man come storming in here last month, accusing me of turning his ex-wife against him after the judge awarded sole custody of their daughter to the mother." She rose from her seat and crossed the room to the filing cabinet in the corner. "Let me see if I have his details for you."

"Have you either seen or heard from this man since his outburst?"

She returned to her seat, wheeled her chair back under her desk and flipped open the file. "No, I haven't received any cause for concern since, but that doesn't mean a thing, does it?"

"You're right, it doesn't. He could have been sitting quiet, hatching a plan to attack a member of your family. I'm not saying that's what has occurred in this case, but it's something we need to consider. Do you have his address on file?"

"Let me see, it should be here somewhere." She flicked

through the relevant notes in the folder and then held up a piece of paper which she handed to Sara.

Sara jotted down the name and address of the man. "Can you tell me anything else about him? Like what he does for a living perhaps?"

"I believe Danny Slater is a mechanic at a large garage in town. I'm sorry, I don't recall the name. Hang on, let me see if I made a note of it in the file." Again, she riffled through the papers but this time sat back in her chair as if defeated. "No good, sorry. I could call his ex-wife, but maybe that would raise too many suspicions, and if he's the one, he might abscond if he knows I've been asking questions. Sorry, I'm probably guilty of thinking ahead and talking nonsense."

"No, you're right to be cautious. We have his name and address, we can go from there. Anyone else you can think of at this stage?"

"No, only him. I suppose there might be others, but I can't think of them at this moment. Once I see my daughter, maybe my head will be somewhat clearer and someone else will come to mind. If so, I'll get in touch with you."

Sara slid one of her business cards across the desk. "Feel free to contact me at any time, day or night."

"I will. Thank you. If there's nothing else, I have a long drive ahead of me."

The three of them rose from their seats.

"There's no need for you to see us out, we'll find our way. Drive carefully, try not to be too distracted during the journey."

"Only time will tell. Don't worry, I'm a safe driver. I'll probably spend most of the time rehearsing what I'm going to say to Kimberley."

Sara nodded, knowing all too well what that experience was like, having done just that on the way there. "Take care. I'll be in touch soon if there are any developments."

"Thank you. I believe in you, Inspector, do your best for us. Hereford has lost a very special person today."

"Don't worry, my team and I will catch the person responsible."

Sara and Carla said farewell to the receptionist on their way out and headed back to the car.

"Where to now? Danny Slater's home?" Carla asked.

"I think it would be pointless. Get onto the station, request that one of the team rings around all the garages in town, see if they can find out where he works. In the meantime, I think we should head over to the medical centre, see what they have to say, if anything."

Carla waited until they had reached the car to make the call. "You do? What's he like?" She raised a thumb when Sara turned her way after pulling onto the main road. "And what garage does he work at, Craig? Thanks, no, I'll fill you in later." She ended the call and said, "Well, that was unexpected. Turns out that Craig knows Danny Slater quite well. Said he's a nice enough chap who services his car at the Hope End Garage on the edge of the city centre."

"I don't recognise the name, do you?"

"I think I've got a rough idea where it is. It's not far, if you fancy doing a U-turn."

Without responding, Sara did just that at the sound of impatient drivers blasting their horns during the manoeuvre.

Carla gasped. "Christ, a bit of warning would have been nice."

Sara chuckled. "I'm a girl on a mission, no time for slacking, you should know that about me by now."

"Yeah, I do. Take the right lane at the top and the first left once we get to the roundabout and we're virtually there."

A few minutes later, Sara drew up on the forecourt of a large garage with four bays, all full. "Must be a busy place. Never knew it existed."

"My ex used to go on about this place. I think a friend of his owns it, or part of it with other partners."

"Your ex? As in the abusive fireman?"

Carla winced. "Couldn't you have just left it there, at an ex?"

"Ouch, that told me. Me and my big mouth, right?"

Carla grinned. "I'll let you off, this time. Don't make a habit of it, though."

"I won't. Consider me told."

They exited the vehicle and entered the small office to the right of the garages. There was an older woman sitting at the desk, typing on a laptop. She was wearing headphones, and Sara had to wave to gain her attention.

"Oh dear, sorry about that, I get carried away. I wear them to block out the noise of the cars revving all day long. It gets to be a bit monotonous at times."

"I bet. No problem." Sara flashed her ID. I was wondering if it would be possible to speak to Danny Slater."

"Ah, you could, if he were here. He's out delivering a car to a customer."

"I see. And where does that customer live?"

"Let me see now, we've got a few of them being delivered today. I'll have to refresh my memory. Here we go, out at Green Crize, he's due back any moment now." She looked out of the window and pointed at a young man getting out of a tow truck on the forecourt. "Seek and he shall appear."

"Can you tell me at what time he left to drop the vehicle off?"

"Around thirty minutes ago, I suppose. I can't say I took that much notice, head down in my work, you know what it's like, working at a busy place like this."

"And what has his schedule been like this morning?"

"I don't understand, has he done something wrong?"

"I don't know. I'm trying to get some basic information about his whereabouts before I speak with him."

"Oh, I see, I think. He showed up before me. I got here at around eight-fifty this morning. He was already working on the car that he had to deliver, making the final tweaks. I took him a cup of coffee; he'd been here since seven-thirty, eager to get the car finished and back to the customer on time. He's very conscientious like that."

"And at around ten this morning, where was he then?"

"I think he popped out for a few minutes, ran along to the café up the road to fetch a bacon sandwich for him and a few of the others. Men rarely perform well on an empty stomach. It's become a habit, dipping out for a sandwich halfway through the morning. What's he supposed to have done to warrant the police showing up here? The boss will be livid if he finds out. He tries to avoid employing men with dubious characters. Sometimes you just can't tell these days, can you?"

"Don't worry, this is us just carrying out enquiries. Would it be okay if we had a quick word with him?"

"I can ask." She dipped out from behind the desk, opened the front door and bellowed, "Danny, in here a second, will you?"

The young man waved and jogged towards the office.

"What about the murder weapon, the car?" Carla whispered in Sara's ear.

"The car that Danny just dropped off, what make was it?" Sara asked, keeping one eye on the approaching young man.

"It was a BMW. Why?"

"It's okay. Thanks for the clarification. Is there another room we can use to hold a private conversation with him?"

"Are you going to take long? Only, the boss will be out for the next twenty minutes or so. I don't suppose he would mind you going in there, providing you don't inconvenience him for too long when he gets back."

"Sounds perfect to me. By what you've already told me, we shouldn't need to hold either of you up for long."

Danny entered the office then. "Susie, what can I do for you?"

"These two ladies would like a quick chat with you, lovely. They're police officers."

He frowned at Sara and Carla. "Police? Have I done something wrong?"

"We don't know." Sara smiled.

"Go through to Mr Chalmers' office, he won't mind," Susie said.

Danny shrugged and opened the door to the office on the right. "Come in, sit down. I won't bother because my overalls are all stained and the boss will throw a fit if he catches me sitting in his chair like this. What can I do for you?"

"What can you tell me about Anne Blake?"

He frowned and chewed on his thumbnail. "The name rings a bell, but I couldn't tell you where I know it from. Is she a customer of ours?"

"No, she is, or should I say was, your wife's solicitor."

"Oh yeah, how stupid of me to forget that. And? Has she made a complaint against me?"

"Not as such. She told us that you caused a bit of a problem a few months back when the judge's ruling in the custody battle went against you."

He held his hands up and shrugged. "And?" he said for the second time. "What about it?"

"You seem pretty chilled about what went on."

"It's called life. I dipped to my lowest ebb, but a group of friends took me out for a drink and kicked my butt, told me it was useless living in the past, expecting things to change. They were right. On to pastures new and all that. Kelly has moved on with her life, too, she's seeing another fella. We all get on great, and I have regular contact with Gemma, despite what the judge ordered."

"So you have no gripes with either your ex-wife or her solicitor then?"

"None whatsoever, and if Blake has told you otherwise, then she's lying to you. For what reason? You'll have to ask her for an answer to that one."

"Can you run through your itinerary this morning?"

He did, and Sara wasn't surprised to find it matched what Susie had told them before Danny had shown up.

Sighing, she smiled at the young man and rose from her chair. "That's good enough for me."

"What is? You haven't told me, not in so many words, what you're doing here, grilling me when I haven't done anything wrong."

"I believe it was a genuine mistake. I'm going to leave it there and apologise for disturbing your working day."

"That's it? No explanation? Only an apology? There must have been a pretty bad reason for you turning up here today to question me. Don't I have a right to know? Seems to me you were about to fling the book at me… albeit by mistake, I hasten to add. If Blake has put me in the frame for something criminal, I think I have a right to know what she's been saying about me."

"I'm not going to divulge what I discussed with her earlier because I don't feel the need to, and Susie has already vouched for your whereabouts this morning. That's good enough for me and lets you off the hook."

"Off the hook? For what? Is Blake all right? Has someone hurt her? Is that why you're here? Because you thought I was capable of hurting that woman, or another human being? I've never had such an accusation flung at me before. It grieves me to believe anyone should think that badly of me. Answer me this, how would you feel if a judge had just snatched your four-year-old out of your grasp? I'm guessing you'd be just as angry as I was at the time, wouldn't you?"

"You're right, I would. I'm sorry, if you must know, Mrs Blake's husband was murdered this morning, that's why we're here to question you."

The colour quickly drained from his face. "What the f...? Jesus, murdered, you say, how?"

"Someone mowed him down with their car."

"Ah, it's all slotting into place now. My name was mentioned, and you thought, he's a mechanic, has got the use of different types of vehicles at his disposal, so it has to be him, am I right?"

"I couldn't possibly comment." Sara issued a slight smile. "As I've already stated, you're in the clear because Susie had already given us your schedule for the day, and you've also confirmed what she told us. Hence my decision not to take the matter further."

"I'm glad. I swear, I could never hurt anyone. You should have seen me at school when the bigger lads wanted to have a fight with me. I'd be the one running to lock myself in the loos."

Sara chuckled. "I used to be pretty much the same when I was younger. Although I always fought my brother's battles, I could never confront any of the girls who picked on me."

"There you go then, you must know how I'm feeling right now. I'm sorry for Mrs Blake's loss but I had nothing to do with it, I can assure you. If I had any issues with her, I would be man enough to go and have it out with her in the open, at her office. I haven't because there was no need to get her involved again."

"I understand. Okay, we'd better get on the road. Thank you for speaking to us today."

"Why wouldn't I? When I have nothing to hide? I hope

you catch the culprit soon. Do you know why he was killed? I know, I shouldn't be asking, it's nothing to do with me."

Sara smiled. "There you go, you've answered your own question perfectly." Her mobile rang in her pocket. "If you'll excuse me, I have to get this."

"Of course."

Sara left the office and exited the main building before she answered the call. "DI Sara Ramsey, how can I help?"

"Inspector Ramsey, it's Anne Blake."

"Hello, Anne. What can I do for you?"

"I'm on my way to Oxford, and I've been mulling over what you said about if anyone had any issues with Hugh, and I think I need you to be aware that he fell out with his brother a few months ago."

"Interesting. Do you think he's likely to want to go further and attempt to kill your husband?"

"I don't know. I wouldn't have thought so, but it would be wrong of me not to mention his name."

"Can you give me a gist as to why they fell out?"

"Trevor is a gambler, he begged us to lend him fifty thousand. Although we both had good jobs, there is no way we'd be able to afford to dish out that kind of money, even if we wanted to. All our money is tied up in the house with a little set aside for Kimberley, should she need it. But his brother doesn't see it that way, and there's no getting through to him either."

"I see. And where are we likely to find Trevor?"

"Hang on, I'll pull onto the hard shoulder and give you his details."

Sara waited patiently until Anne spoke again.

"Here you are. It's flat three, seventy Ferndale Road. It's a house that has been renovated into six flats, set back from the road, so be careful you don't miss it."

"Thanks. Is he likely to be there during the day or does he work?"

"He's what he would call 'between jobs' at present."

"I see, I think I understand where this is heading now. Okay, leave it with us. If we can track him down today, we'll ask the relevant questions. How are you holding up?"

"I'm fine, better than I thought I would be in the circumstances. I'm trying to hold it together, if only to get me to Oxford in one piece."

"Have you contacted your daughter at all?"

"No, I thought it would be best if I showed up there, otherwise she'll twig something is wrong if I contact her out of the blue. We usually wait for her to call us, you know what teenagers are like with their privacy."

"I can imagine. All right, I'll let you get on. I'll give you a call back later if anything develops with Trevor."

"Thanks. I feel bad putting him in the frame like this but… I need to know who murdered my husband and why."

"Quite right, too. Drive safely."

"Thank you. I will."

Sara ended the call and turned to face Carla. "Interesting development."

"It could be. Want to pop round there and see if he's in?"

"I think we should. We can call to Hugh's place of work afterwards."

THE BUILDING WAS an impressive Georgian style, not the kind of place an unemployed person would likely rent, but then, what did Sara know about that sort of thing?

She rang the bell to flat three, but there was no answer. She tried to open the outer door, but it was locked. So she rang the bell for flat four, hoping the tenant would let them in. There was no reply there either. "We're out of luck. We'll call back later. Will you ring the station for me, see if Trevor Blake has any kind of record? It'll give us something to go on if he has."

Carla made the call once they were back in the car and remained on the line while Christine checked the system. She put her phone on speaker.

"Nothing showing up, Carla. Is there anything else you need me to check?"

Carla glanced Sara's way. "Is there?"

"No, I can't think of anything right now. We'll get back to you if that changes, Christine, thanks."

"Okay, I'm here if you need me."

"Wait, yes, while we're out and about, can you sort out the background checks on the victim and his family for us?" Sara said, changing her mind. "Hugh Blake, his wife is Anne Blake, she's a solicitor in the city. I don't think we'll find anything, the wife has just told us that all their money is tied up in the property, but it would be negligent of us if we didn't do the necessary digging."

"I hear you, boss. Leave it with me."

"Hopefully, we'll be back soon. We've got an alert on the car. Will you ask Barry and Craig to sort through any footage available in the area? I don't think there will be much because the incident happened a long way outside the city limits, but maybe trace the car through the ANPRs and go from there."

"I'll pass the message on. Good luck."

"Thanks, we're going to need it. It's already proving to be a frustrating case, and we're still only a couple of hours into the investigation."

"You'll get there, boss, you always do."

"I wish I had your faith, Christine. It's severely lacking so far. See you later." Sara nodded for Carla to end the call.

"You sound down," Carla noted.

"Perhaps a little. We've not got a lot to go on so far, that's the annoying part."

"Hey, not so. We've got the car and a good view of the driver. We can always carry out a lineup, should the need arise."

"Haven't had to resort to having one of those for a while. They always reek of desperation in my book."

"You're nuts. Blimey, in the good old days, they used to happen every day or so, didn't they? According to the research I was conducting last week."

"Research? For what?"

"Just research."

Sara frowned and shot Carla a swift look and then concentrated on her driving once more. "Why the secrecy? Are you up to something?"

"Not at all. All right then, it's something Des and I like to do in the evening."

"What? You've lost me."

Tutting, Carla said, "Delve into old crimes, some that have remained unsolved, and analyse what went wrong with the investigation."

"Wow, seriously? That's pretty in-depth stuff, even for you. Why not go home and veg out in front of the TV like normal people do?"

"Charming. Because it's what we enjoy doing. Admittedly, it's only since I've been with Des that I've considered doing it, but don't knock something you haven't tried. It's pretty cool and definitely gives our brain cells a workout at the end of a long day."

"That's my point, though. Your job, both of you, is hard enough as it is without you putting yourselves through it at home. Your brain needs a rest, time to recover."

"If you say so. It's not like I'm saying we're up all night, delving into all the nooks and crannies of the cases... we

enjoy it. Are you saying that you believe it might be detrimental to the way I work alongside you during the day?"

"Now you're guilty of putting words into my mouth."

"Can we change the subject? I sense we're both getting
unnecessarily worked up about this. Maybe I should have
kept my mouth shut to begin with."

"Where did that come from? Let's not fall out over something so insignificant, Carla."

"I'm not, you are. What's wrong with having a hobby you
enjoy that is job related?"

Sara cringed. "Nothing at all. Let's call a halt to the
conversation now before one of us says something she will
regret."

Carla folded her arms and puffed out a breath then
turned to look out of the passenger window, leaving Sara
feeling helpless.

The tension hung in the air between them for the rest of
the journey to the medical centre.

Before getting out of the car, Sara faced her partner. "Hey,
can we call a truce? I hate it when we fall out. I didn't mean
to sound disrespectful about the choices you make. I suppose
your admission came as a shock."

"Yes, okay. Everyone has to have their own interests in
this life. This happens to be mine at the moment. Who's to
say whether that will change next month or next year?"

Sara held her little finger out. "Friends again?"

Carla reluctantly gripped her finger with her own pinkie
and shook it. "Of course."

"Right, now that's out of the way, let's get back on track
with the investigation and see what his colleagues have to
say."

They entered the smart building, adjacent to the railway
station and opposite Morrisons supermarket. Sara could
smell the newness of the carpets and furniture; that's the first

thing that hit her when they walked through the glass-fronted reception area.

"Maybe I should consider changing my surgery. This is pretty swanky, isn't it?"

"I was thinking the same. Depends on how the doctors treat their patients at the end of the day, doesn't it?"

"True."

There were two receptionists on duty behind the curved counter.

Sara flashed her warrant card. "Hi, is it possible to speak to the person in charge? Would that be a head doctor or practice manager, perhaps?"

"Oh, yes. That will be Miss Nightingale. I'll give her a shout for you. May I ask what it's concerning?"

Sara smiled. "I'll let her know when I speak with her."

The slender woman swept her long hair over her shoulder and marched off to an office behind her. She returned moments later with a woman in her fifties, wearing a suit that was clearly too tight for her in places.

"Hello, you wanted to see me? May I ask why?"

"In private would be better, Miss Nightingale."

"Very well. Come round. We'll go into my office. Did you want a drink?"

"No, thanks," Sara replied.

She and Carla wound their way around the reception desk and followed the woman into her office which over-looked a pretty courtyard at the rear.

"Please, won't you take a seat?"

They sat, and Sara studied the woman, her mind not quite made up about her as yet.

"We're sorry to interrupt, we appreciate how busy you are."

"Then why have you?" Miss Nightingale asked the instant Sara paused to take a breath.

"We're conducting inquiries into an incident that happened earlier today and wondered if you, or any of your colleagues, could shed any light on the subject."

"An incident, you say? What might that consist of?" She interlinked her hands on the desk in front of her and sat upright in her plush executive chair.

"I'm getting to that."

Miss Nightingale raised an eyebrow as if to say, 'Well? I'm waiting'.

"Earlier today, we were called to a major crime scene involving a member of your practice."

"What? Who? I don't have the faintest idea what you're going on about. You're going to have to be a lot clearer than that, Inspector, if you're seeking my help."

"Okay. Dr Hugh Blake lost his life this morning, outside his home."

Sara watched as the high colour drained from the woman's cheeks.

"My goodness, no, tell me it isn't true, not Hugh."

"I'm sorry, it is true. We've already informed his wife of his passing, hence why we're here now."

"I still don't understand." Miss Nightingale seemed perplexed or even shellshocked by the revelation. "He was such a good doctor who truly cared about his patients. Can I ask how he died? You said he lost his life, how?"

"Unfortunately, we believe he was intentionally murdered."

"I can't believe this. Do you know why?" Miss Nightingale fidgeted in her seat and glanced around the room.

"Are you okay?" Sara asked, curious as to why the woman was behaving in such a way.

"I can't explain it. It's as if someone has just walked over my grave. I'm sensitive to people passing."

"Sensitive? As in you can communicate with the dead?"

"No, not as such. I've had it before, when I've lost a family member. I get a sudden gust of wind or breeze if you like. Forget it, it's a feeling best ignored."

"Were you close to Hugh?"

"Not in that sense. We've been work colleagues for several years."

"How many years?"

"Around ten, maybe eleven. We were all so excited when this place was opened, it was a new beginning for a lot of us. I'm so sad that he's no longer with us. How did he die, did you say? I can't remember."

"No, I didn't. Someone ran him down outside his home this morning."

Miss Nightingale's head jutted forward. "What? Why? That's unthinkable that someone should do that. Who did it, do you know?"

"We've got a description of the car which we've circulated, but as to why the attack happened, we were hoping someone around here would be able to fill in the blanks for us."

"Around here? I don't understand, how would we know?"

"As his colleagues, maybe he hinted at something that was possibly bothering him. Maybe someone had reached out to him and he'd turned his back on them."

Miss Nightingale thrust her shoulders back and wagged a finger. "Are you talking about a patient doing this to Hugh?"

"It's a consideration. It has to be at this early stage, it's all we have to go on."

"Jesus, I've heard it all now. There is no way on earth that would happen. You clearly didn't know Hugh as a person. He was loved by every member of the team and he had a patient list that used to grow monthly. I find it incredulous that you would dare to think that one of our patients, here at the practice, could be guilty of carrying out such a cruel and heartless act."

Sara hitched up a shoulder. "Until other evidence or suggestions come our way, then I'm afraid that's all we have to go on."

Shaking her head, Miss Nightingale tutted. "What else can I say? You can't expect me to believe we have a murderer on our books as a patient."

Sara raised an eyebrow. "Well, someone went out of their way to kill him. Unless you can come up with a suitable alternative."

"Of course I can't. You've already spoken to his wife, Anne, did you ask her? Wait just a second… yes, I found Hugh quite distant in the staffroom one day a few weeks ago. I asked him why he was looking so troubled, and he told me he had personal problems with a family member."

Sara's interest spiked at the revelation. "Did he say who?"

"No. And, as I'm not generally a nosey person, I didn't push him further. I simply told him I was there if he needed someone to talk to about it. He was a private man in that respect, so I gave him the space to work out his problems."

"And did he?" Sara asked. She had an inkling whom Miss Nightingale was referring to, given the conversation she'd recently had with the victim's wife.

"What? Work through the problem?" she asked, and Sara nodded. "I think so. I only caught him off-guard once. Whether he was more cautious about how openly he displayed his feelings after that, well, I suppose we'll never know, will we? I can't believe we're sat here discussing this and that he's… now dead. How do people get over such a shock when a colleague, a valued member of a thriving practice such as this, has gone?"

"I'm not saying it's going to be easy, but you will get over it. I suppose reflecting on the good times you've had together over the years will eventually help in the end."

"I hope so. I feel numb, as if I've just left the dentist's chair after having several extractions. Purely and simply numb, and it's a dreadful feeling to try and overcome, I can assure you."

"It's going to take time. Would it be possible to speak to your colleagues, see if they can come up with anything different to you?"

"You can do what you like, within reason. You need to bear in mind that we're running a very busy practice here, so if you are prepared to work around that significant issue then, yes, by all means, feel free to chat with people. On duty at the moment, we have two receptionists, four doctors and three nurses, plus we're inundated with patient appointments."

"I know this is asking a lot but is it possible for you to organise the interviews according to people's commitments?"

"It might take me a few minutes to sort out. What am I saying? It is going to take me a while to work it out for you."

"Take all the time you need."

"Follow me back to the reception area. I can get one of the girls to set up one of the consultation rooms as an interview room for you."

"We can't thank you enough for accommodating us like this."

The three of them rose from their seats and left the office.

Miss Nightingale had a brief chat with the two receptionists on duty, and they all put their heads together whilst consulting the screen of one of the computers.

Eventually, Miss Nightingale showed them into a consultation room off to the left and slid a list of names across the desk to Sara. "There you go. I've got a copy as well. Unless anything untoward should crop up, which is likely knowing the day-to-day running of this place and the way some patients fail to contact us at short notice to cancel an appointment... anyway, if all goes according to plan, we should have this wrapped up within a couple of hours. Now, can I get you both a drink before I arrange for the first person to come and see you?"

"You've been super-efficient already, why stop now?" Sara smiled and sat in one of the chairs. "Two white coffees with one sugar. Thank you for your kindness," she felt she needed to add at the end.

"My pleasure. If you go away from here today with a clearer image of what may have led to Hugh's death, then I'll be utterly thrilled. Ouch, wrong choice of words."

Sara held up a hand. "Don't worry, we get what you meant. Fingers crossed, eh?"

OVER THE NEXT three hours to be exact, they questioned every member of staff available on site. All of whom praised the way Hugh Blake had dealt with his patients. They described him as one of the most caring doctors they had ever come across, who never raised his voice at any of his colleagues and definitely never to a member of the public. But not one person was able to point them in the right direction of any ill-feeling towards Blake.

At the end of the interviews, Sara and Carla thanked Miss Nightingale for looking after them so well and left the practice. By now, time was getting on, and the traffic was hectic after the schools had finished for the day.

Carla suspected that Sara wasn't returning to the station and asked, "Are you going back to Trevor's flat?"

"We might as well. Hopefully, enough time has passed and

he'll be at home now. If he's still absent, then we'll call it a day and return to base."

"Makes sense to me. Who do you believe is behind Hugh's death?"

Sara blew out a breath and then drew in a couple of deeper ones. "You tell me. Nothing is coming to mind, except the brother. We'll soon see if that's worth pursuing or not, I hope."

The traffic was horrendous throughout the city, and by the time Sara pulled up outside the Georgian-style flats once more, her nerves were wrought and jangling with frustration. "Jesus, this city gets worse and worse. There's just nowhere for the traffic to go. Roll on building that bypass."

"Ouch! Really, you're going to have the conservationists stringing you up if you say that too loud in a public area."

"Times move on. Something has to give. These roads weren't built to handle the extortionate amount of traffic that we have today."

"Get you. I bet councillors in every town and city between Land's End and John O'Groats are saying the same, day in, day out. These days there are far more vehicles on the roads, dare I say adding to the pollution and ruining Earth's atmosphere as well."

"Yeah, okay, it's called the snowball effect, isn't it? And I think we should stop right there before we both go too far."

They exited the car and walked towards the flats. Over to their right, a dark car came to a standstill in one of the allocated parking spaces.

"Could be him," Carla whispered.

"We'll see. What type of car is he driving, can you see?"

"It's a Ford, I believe."

"Not what I wanted to hear. He's spotted us, brace yourself."

"I've got my hand on my pepper spray and I won't be afraid to use it."

"Great, thanks, partner."

The man stopped, and Sara flashed her ID as they approached him.

"Trevor Blake?"

"Yes. You're the police? Was I speeding or something?"

"Not as far as we're aware. Would it be convenient to have a chat with you, inside?"

"Not until you tell me why."

"We're investigating a major crime that took place earlier."

He inclined his head. "And what does that have to do with me?"

"Your name cropped up during our enquiries."

"You're pulling my plonker, aren't you? You have to be. Who would throw my name into the hat? And what the bloody hell am I supposed to have done? And, furthermore, no, I'm not letting you anywhere near my flat. You can't force me to let you in either. I know my rights, lady."

"It's inspector. You're correct, you have rights, but then we also have the right to interview you if your name has come to light during our investigation."

"We'll soon see about that. I'm calling my solicitor." He fished his mobile out of his pocket and huffed and puffed while he scrolled through the screen. "Damn, where is it? Ah yes, here it is. Do I call him, or are you going to tell me what this is all about? The choice is yours. Innocent until proven guilty… just throwing that one in there, in case it has slipped your mind."

"Would you care to join us in the back of our car?"

"Not really. I know what you coppers get up to, fitting innocent folks like me up. I can see the grim determination in your eyes."

53

Sara couldn't help herself, she burst out laughing at the man's over-the-top remark. "I'm sorry you feel like that. Look, we can either take this inside, or if you'd rather, we can continue this conversation down at the station."

"Like fuck we can. Why should I go with you when you haven't even got the decency to tell me what this is all about?"

The long day catching up on her, Sara shrugged and sighed. "No problem, we can do it here. All I was trying to do was save you the embarrassment of conducting a police interview where your neighbours are likely to overhear. All good for me."

"Get on with it. Like I give two hoots what they're likely to say anyway. I'm packing up and getting ready to move on. Oops, maybe I shouldn't have let that slip."

Sara smiled. "Noted. Don't worry. Where were you between the hours of nine-thirty and ten-thirty this morning?"

His brow wrinkled. "On my way to Worcester. Why?"

"What time did you get on the road?"

"Around nine-fifteen. There was a holdup just outside Worcester. A lorry had spread its load over the B-road, held the traffic up. Almost made us late, it did."

"Us?"

"Yes, me and a couple of friends went to Worcester races today."

"Ah, an all-day affair then, I should think. Am I right?"

"Totally. Not worth going all that way to cheer on a few horses in a couple of races, might as well make it a day trip. Why? What are you investigating, or aren't you allowed to tell me?"

"In that case, you won't mind supplying us with the names of your friends so we can check out your alibi, will you?"

"I'm not giving you any such information, not until you open up to me."

"Very well. This morning, at around ten, someone killed your brother."

"My what? Are you talking about Hugh here?"

"Do you have another brother?"

"No, it was a stupid question, ignore me. Damn, how? Why?"

"The why is what we've spent all day trying to ascertain. The how is, he was mowed down outside his house, and the culprit drove off not long after."

"But I don't understand… my next question has to be why you've come here to see me? Hang on, you said someone had given you my name. Why? To frame me for his murder?"

"Not really. During our enquiries, we asked the inevitable question to see if Hugh had fallen out with anyone lately who might then have a grudge with him."

"It's all making sense now. You've been speaking to Anne, haven't you? That bitch has always had it in for me."

"Initially, your name didn't come to mind. It wasn't until a few hours after we broke the news to her that she got back to us and told us that you had recently fallen out with your brother regarding a money issue. Is that true?"

"Yes, I'm not going to stand here and deny it, what would be the point? However, what I am going to tell you is that I would never, not in a million years, lay a finger on my brother, as much as I've been tempted to in the past. Let alone sodding well kill him." He ran a hand through his greying hair and puffed out his fleshy cheeks. "This is a bitter pill to swallow, especially if my sister-in-law has thrown my name into the mix."

"She hasn't, not really. If you have a suitable alibi then that should be the end of the matter. I can see you're visibly shaken by the news."

"Christ on a skateboard, wouldn't you be if a copper showed up outside your gaff and accused you of killing your own brother?"

"You have a point, not that I did that. Forgive me for trying to do my job, of trying to find your brother's killer."

"All right, there's no need for you to get snarky with me. Were there any witnesses?"

"Yes, Hugh's neighbour, Lucy, saw the whole thing."

"Poor her. Did she take note of the reg of the car?"

"Sadly not. We've issued an alert for the vehicle."

He shook his head. "I bet you've got diddly squat hope of finding it."

"We're not defeatists, far from it," Sara replied.

"I still don't get why you've shown up on my doorstep. I don't get it. What am I missing?" His eyes narrowed and then widened again. "You don't think I had a hand in it, like got someone to kill him? Paid someone to do it?"

Sara's gaze latched on to his. "Is that a possibility?"

"You tell me. No, I'll tell you—no, it's categorically not. As to the money I asked Hugh for, I managed to tap a friend up in London, he lent it to me in the end."

"What, so you can continue your gambling habit?"

"Is that an offence? If you must know, I won big a few weeks back and paid him half his money back. There are highs and lows to everything in this life, even gambling, you're not always on a losing streak. Now, if you don't mind, I'm eager to get on with my packing. I move out at the end of the week."

"Where are you moving to?"

"Around the corner. Don't tell me, you want the address."

Sara smiled. "You read my mind."

He willingly dictated his new address, and Carla jotted it down in her notebook which told Sara all she needed to know about him, that he couldn't have possibly killed his own brother, he'd been far too open and honest with them up to now. She recognised the address so knew he wasn't trying to pull a fast one on them.

"Thanks. Now we need the numbers of your friends who attended the races with you today."

"What the fuck? You wouldn't put me through that, would you? I suppose you're going to tell them why I need an alibi as well?"

"No, we would never reveal the facts about an ongoing case with strangers. Hand over their details, and we'll contact them now and it'll all be done and dusted in a matter of minutes, then, and only then, we'll let you get on with your day."

"Gee, thanks, that's pretty magnanimous of you."

Sara grinned. "I'm nothing but fair, I assure you."

He sought out his friends' details in his phone and reeled off the numbers for Carla to make a note of. There were five in total. Then he returned his phone to his jacket pocket and folded his arms. "Now what?"

"Why don't you wait in your car while we make the calls?"

He harumphed and turned on his heel, slamming the driver's door once he'd jumped in behind the steering wheel.

"Shit! If looks could kill," Sara grumbled.

"What's your gut feeling telling you about him?"

"That he's got nothing to do with his brother's death. However, we, or should I say I, have been wrong in the past and regretted my decision not to act upon the facts when they've openly presented themselves."

"I can vouch for that in not more than two instances over the years, and they were dubious to the extreme. Don't beat yourself up, Sara."

"Let's get on with the chore. I'm eager to get back to base and then go home at a reasonable hour."

Carla held her pad open, and they took it in turns to

choose a number from the list. All five friends gave the exact same times, or thereabouts, and cited the holdup that had occurred to disrupt their outing without even pausing to contemplate the answer. Satisfied, Sara told Carla to go back to the car while she had a word with Trevor. She stood alongside the driver's door and gestured for him to lower his window. He did, slowly.

"Good news, they backed up your account, so that's my job completed here."

"Shame you weren't prepared to take my word for it, instead of causing me a sackful of embarrassment. They'll be hounding me for answers the next time we meet up."

"I can't do any more than apologise. I'm sure you'll get over it. Thanks for your time."

"What? Is that it? I suppose you're going to tell me to keep my distance from Annie now, right?"

"Not really. You have a right to offer her your condolences at an appropriate time. Anyway, she's travelling down to break the awful news to her daughter at the university."

"Shit! I don't envy her that job."

"My advice would be to just be there, if she needs you, without causing her too much stress."

He rolled his eyes and sighed. "I suppose I'd better break the news to our mother, she's down in London in a nursing home with early onset dementia."

"If you think that's wise. How bad is she?"

"She has her moments. Neither of us felt we could cope with the care she would have needed on a daily basis, so we decided to sell her house and use the proceeds to fund the rest of her stay in the home. Who knows how long that's going to be? Families don't stand a chance of getting any inheritance from their loved ones, not these days. Another black mark against the Tories' policies. Don't get me started on that one."

Sara smiled and nodded. "I hear you. By what I've gathered today, do you really think any inheritance due to you wouldn't have ended up in the hands of a bookie?"

"Harsh, Inspector, very harsh. I would have put most of it towards buying a new house."

"Ah, right. You say that now, until the urge strikes, eh? Anyway, I sense we'd be going round in circles for hours if we continued this conversation. I must get back to it, I have a killer to find."

"Dare I wish you good luck, or is saying it tempting fate?"

"You can say it. My team and I will be giving the investigation everything we have and more."

"That's good to hear."

"I'll leave you my card in case anything comes to mind regarding your brother or if you happen to hear anything to do with his death."

He took the card from her and slipped it into his inside jacket pocket. "Thanks, not sure that's likely."

Sara returned to the car and drove back to the station.

"Any news, team?"

"Ah, there you are, ma'am. No, we were hoping to have news about the car but nothing has shown up so far."

Sara sank into the chair behind her. "Shit! Did you manage to track it at all on the cameras?"

"Partially, or should I say fleetingly."

Sara's mood brightened, if cautiously. "I don't suppose you got a look at the driver, did you?"

"No, sorry, boss, can't say I did."

"Great, so we're back to square one, not getting anywhere fast." Her gaze drifted to the other side of the room to Christine. "How about the background checks, anything shown up there?"

Christine's demeanour was grim. "Sorry, boss. I was hoping to share better news with you upon your return."

"Not to worry. I sense this case is going to have us tugging our hair out several times over, folks. Let's not get downhearted about it, all we can do is our very best. We need to hang on to the hope of finding that car. At the moment, it's all we have." Sara left her seat and walked over to the whiteboard which she brought up to date with the details they had learnt while they'd been out, then she called for the team's attention and ran through what they had discovered.

"Where do we begin on this one, boss?" Craig asked. He crossed his arms and shook his head.

"Unfortunately, I'm still trying to figure that one out for myself. With very little to go on, I sense we're going to have a tough few weeks ahead of us. So we're going to need to give it our all."

"Could this be more about the wife than the husband?" Jill asked.

"Possibly. It seems more likely, given their careers, but who knows? I'd rather not concentrate on one angle at the risk of limiting our expertise. So let's keep an open mind on this one for now."

"It wouldn't harm doing some extra digging on the wife, though, would it?" Carla suggested. "You know, discreetly."

"I think we should. When we interviewed everyone at the surgery, I didn't get the impression that anything was likely to come our way from down there, but I've been known to be wrong before and would prefer keeping an open mind on that for now. Okay, I think we should call it a day and start over again tomorrow with fresh minds."

The team switched off their computers and said their farewells as they drifted off for the day.

"You seem down in the mouth, are you all right?" Carla asked.

"I'm fine. Desperately trying not to let the frustration take hold, it's far too early for that to happen. You get off. I'll tidy my desk and then I think I'm going to drop by the mortuary, see if Lorraine has anything for us. I want to check in on her anyway, she sounded stressed earlier."

"Can't you leave that until the morning?"

"No, something is telling me that I need to go there this evening. I can't pinpoint what it is but I'd be kicking myself if I got all the way home and didn't satisfy my urge to make sure she was okay. There was definitely something on her mind earlier today."

"If you think it's the right thing to do. I'd be inclined to take a step back for now. She knows where you are if she needs you."

"Ordinarily, I would agree with you, but you know what it's like when the draw becomes too much."

"Ah, I get where you're going with this. You think it might be detrimental to the case if she's not on top of her game."

Sara winked and tapped the side of her nose. "There, I knew you'd cotton on, eventually."

"In that case, I'll leave you to it and wish you luck with your endeavours. Lorraine isn't the easiest of people to handle, even if she has become a good friend of yours over the years."

"I'm not expecting miracles, however, it would be wrong of me to cast her aside if she was in need of my help."

"Agreed. See you in the morning."

"Good luck with your research," Sara shouted after her.

Carla made her way to the door and held up a hand in a half-hearted wave.

CHAPTER 3

*T*he closer Sara got to Lorraine's office the more butterflies appeared to take off and circulate in her empty stomach. It was then that she realised that neither she nor Carla had found time to eat during their busy day.

It just means that I'll appreciate my evening meal all the more, hopefully.

She travelled the length of the long grey corridor and stopped a few feet from Lorraine's office when she heard her friend let out a moan and something hit the floor. Worried, Sara upped her pace and appeared in Lorraine's office doorway not long after.

"Jesus fucking Christ, you scared the frigging crap out of me. What are you doing here?" Lorraine glanced at the clock on the wall beside her. "And at this hour? Shouldn't you be at home, cuddling up to that dishy hubby of yours?"

"I'm on my way, thought I'd stop off and have a quick chat with you first. Anything wrong?"

Lorraine picked up the file she had dropped on the floor and twiddled with her pen, pushing the button on top down repeatedly, annoying Sara. "I'm fine."

Sara entered the room and took a seat opposite her friend. "Stop trying to kid a kidder, what's up?"

Lorraine sat back in her chair and then immediately bolted upright again. "I can't burden you with this."

"With what? Let me be the judge of whether it's a burden or not. Come on, what's on your mind?"

Lorraine hesitated and then placed her elbows on the table and covered her face with her hands.

"Come on, love. You're scaring me now."

She dropped her hands and stared at Sara. "I didn't mean to. This is such a difficult one to process."

"What is? A problem shared and all that."

"I know. I simply don't know where to begin."

"I usually find from the beginning is a good a start as any. Give it a try, hon. I'm in no hurry, Mark will understand."

"Are you sure about this?"

"Yep. Would you rather get out of here and discuss it at the pub instead?"

"No, here's fine. Okay, a few days ago, I got a call from an old friend of mine, a doctor who works at the hospital in A and E."

"Blimey, and there was me thinking you didn't have much of a social life and I was the only person you knew well enough to be called a friend."

Sara chuckled at the quip, but Lorraine sat there stony-faced.

"Are you going to allow me to tell you this story or not?"

Sara slapped the back of her hand. "Sorry, my bad. Go on. Straight-faced now and eager to hear."

Lorraine hesitated for a while as if searching for the right words to continue with her story.

"Come on, it can't be that bad, Lorraine. This isn't like you at all. What gives?"

Inhaling a large breath, Lorraine dropped the pen and

63

interlinked her fingers. She twisted them one hundred and eighty degrees and back before she spoke again. "Right, Joel alerted me to a patient's death that was of grave concern to him. A woman who was only fifty-nine had suffered from a heart attack and died while the paramedics were about to transport her to the hospital to get treatment."

"That's a shame. Isn't that more common than we realise, though? People dying en route to hospital, especially with the service being stretched to its max right now?"

"Possibly. However, it was the reaction of the woman's son he was more concerned about."

Sara tilted her head. "What was that?"

"Very over the top. He was her full-time carer and had been for around five years. The woman was disabled several years ago."

"Okay. So what did your doctor friend need from you?"

"For me to carry out a post-mortem."

"Ouch, can you do that? For a simple heart attack?"

"It's usual in circumstances such as this one."

"And was there? Something inappropriate?"

"Yes. It took a while to discover it, but when I found it, everything kind of slotted into place."

Frowning, her head too full of her ongoing case to even consider what Lorraine could be driving at, Sara queried, "Meaning? I'm tired, you're going to have to spoon-feed me this one, mate, because my brain cells appear to have shut down for the evening."

"Figures. Typical copper." Lorraine tried to joke her way out of the situation but failed. "There are certain things a person can do to another person that can bring on a heart attack, in case you haven't realised."

"Go on, such as?"

"The initial tests I carried out on the woman's organs came back inconclusive, so I ran further in-depth tests, and that's when the answer hit me. She was poisoned. Not all in one go, I think it has been going on a while, small quantities that wouldn't be noticed when questioned. If you get where I'm coming from."

Sara inched to the edge of her seat. "You think the son has been poisoning her for some time?"

"So it would seem. I have a theory that perhaps he didn't mean it to go too far and he gave her too much which more than likely induced the heart attack. Joel, my friend, said the man's reaction was, well… he overreacted, it's as simple as that."

"Had she had a heart attack at home nothing further would have been done, is that what you're saying?"

"Possibly."

"But if he was poisoning her, why would he bother to call the ambulance in the first place?"

"That's what I'm struggling to figure out. Maybe he changed his mind, didn't want her to go so soon. Perhaps he's a sadistic bastard who wanted her to hang around longer, enjoying the fact that she was suffering before his very eyes."

"That's some notion you've conjured up there."

"That's what is driving me crazy. I keep asking myself if I'm doing the man an injustice."

Sara wagged her finger. "Oh no you don't, don't even go there, not if it's as you say it is, that she's been poisoned. You can't feel sorry for the bastard. His overreaction was probably because he never expected to get caught out. He has been, end of. What are you going to do about it?"

"I don't know."

"What? I know this is an informal chat, but you know you have to do the right thing and take things further."

Lorraine stared at her and offered up the faintest of smiles. "Would you be willing to take the case on? I know you're under the cosh right now with your new investigation and I'm asking a lot of you but… I wouldn't feel right handing the case over to someone else. You get me?"

"Yeah, I do, and sometimes that's a massive downfall of mine."

Lorraine's expression changed from pleading to one of hurt.

"Just kidding. Can I think about it overnight and get back to you in the morning? Our new case could grind to a halt before it's got off the ground. If it does, then my team and I can pick up the slack on this one, if you're sure it's a case that needs delving into."

"I'm sure. He came here, the son. He wasn't a happy bunny. I know members of the public who have lost a loved one can react in different ways, but he was keen to come down heavily on me for performing the PM without his permission."

"Christ, I hope you told him where to get off?"

"Sort of. I ended up having to ask him to leave. He refused. I had to call security to escort him off the premises. He tore past me and into the fridge area, began tearing open all the drawers to find his mother."

"Shit! Did he manage to find her?"

"Yes, eventually. I tried my very best to keep him away from her, stood in front of several of the other drawers, hoping he'd think I was trying to prevent him from getting to her, but he wasn't easily fooled and continued to open the other ones. When he found her…"

"What happened? You can't stop there."

"Again, his reaction wasn't what I was expecting at all. He just froze, staring at her. Taking in every inch of her stark-white face and blue lips with tears streaming down his cheeks."

"Guilt?"

Lorraine shrugged. "I wish I knew. I've never doubted myself so much as I have in the past few days."

Sara shook her head. "This is so unlike you. The evidence is speaking for itself, isn't it?"

"I'm not so sure. One minute I think it has to be him, but then, on the flip side, I keep telling myself that he wouldn't, no, he couldn't have done it."

"But why? It all seems very clear-cut to me."

Lorraine's frown deepened. "Why come here? Why did he want to see her?"

"He's a sadist. Maybe he wanted to see the results of his actions a final time."

"But he's been here, or tried to get in a few times since."

"What? If you feel threatened... Jesus, why didn't you tell me?"

"That's just it, I don't, not personally. I told you, I'm struggling what to make of things, I'm so confused."

Lorraine placed her hands over her face, and for the first time in years, Sara saw how broken she was.

She tore out of her seat and rounded the desk to comfort her friend, flinging an arm around her shoulder and pulling her close.

"Don't show me any sympathy, it'll only make me a darn sight worse."

"Don't be daft, as if I'd let you go through this all alone. Why don't you come home with me? Mark can spoil us both tonight."

"As appealing as that idea sounds, I have another two PMs to perform this evening before I leave. I was in the process of clearing my mind ready to cut open the first one when you descended upon me."

"Then come afterwards. It doesn't matter to me. I'm concerned about you."

"You worry too much. I'll be fine."

Sara released her arms and took a step back. "So why has this got to you so much?"

Lorraine chewed on her lip for several seconds and admitted, "I think probably because it's the anniversary of my mother's death coming up. I don't often dwell on it, but for some reason, she's been on my mind a lot recently."

"I'm so sorry to hear that. It's hard when they go. There's not a day goes by when I don't think of my mum."

"I didn't mean to be so insensitive, it's only been about a year since your mum went."

"You're not being insensitive at all."

"How's your dad's new relationship working out?"

"He's fine. I'm glad to see he has a smile on his face most days, even if Lesley isn't too happy about him having a new love in his life."

"She doesn't count, does she?"

Sara walked around the other side of the desk. "I keep telling her that, but you know how stubborn she can be."

"I do, well… from what you've told me anyway."

"She's going to have to get used to her. I don't think Margaret will be going anywhere soon. Anyway, I think she's been the tonic Dad needed to cope with Mum's loss. It might not be everyone's cup of tea, getting into bed with another woman so soon after losing your devoted wife, if you get what I mean, but it was a necessary energiser for my dad. If I'm honest with you, I dread to think what might have happened to him if he hadn't hooked up with his new love."

"It's lovely to see, at his time of life. I see only too often the damage a broken heart can cause in the elderly. Right, I haven't got time to spend chatting with you all evening, I have PMs to perform."

"Before you head off to the theatre, can you give me this chap's details, and Carla and I will pay him a visit first thing in the morning?"

Lorraine picked up her pen and scribbled down Paul Hanson's address and slid it across the table towards Sara. "There you go. Be careful."

"Don't worry about me, I'm the one who is concerned about you. Be extra cautious tonight when you leave, all right?"

"I will. Drive home safely."

"Are you sure I can't persuade you to come and stay with us? Mark will be in his element, fussing over two beautiful women."

They both laughed.

"As tempting as that sounds, honestly, I'm fine. I prefer to stick with my home comforts, you know how it is."

"I do. I'll get out of your hair then. Any problems, give me a ring, okay?"

"I promise. Now go home and have a lovely evening with that gorgeous husband of yours."

Sara jogged round the desk again and gave Lorraine a peck on the cheek and a crushing hug. "Call me when you get home, it doesn't matter what time it is."

"I'll text you, but there's really no need. You're blowing all this up out of proportion. Now shoo!"

Sara trotted over to the door and blew her friend a kiss, then ran up the hallway back to the car. She took in her surroundings whilst she made her way to her vehicle.

The area is well lit, so maybe Lorraine is right, I'm being over-cautious and guilty of suffocating her.

On the way home, her thoughts returned to her sister, and she decided to give her a call. "Hey, sis. How's it going?"

"Long time no hear," Lesley bit back churlishly.

"You know how it is, busy bee."

"You've found the time to get in touch with Dad and to visit him quite often, though, and that new bit of skirt of his."

"Lesley," she warned. "Give them a break. She's really nice, if you take the trouble to get to know her."

"I feel like an outcast. You've had more to do with her than I have."

Sara briefly closed her eyes. They flew open a second later when she realised she was still driving. "And whose fault is that? Either you put in the effort or you're going to feel excluded, because you will be."

Lesley remained silent for a few moments. "I don't want her in our lives. Mum's barely cold in her grave, and what does Dad do? Bring another woman home for us to get used to. How dare he?"

"That's not fair. He was alone for a few months first. Why shouldn't he have companionship at his age? Who are we to prevent him from finding future happiness?"

"It's just wrong. All wrong the way he went about it. Introducing her to us like that, without even mentioning her to either of us."

"He was probably too scared to. Can you blame him? Considering what your reaction has been to the news after all this time?"

"She'll never replace Mum, not in my eyes."

"I'm sure she realises that. I haven't seen any indication that she's trying to do that at all. And yes, I've put the effort in and spent a fair bit of time with her over the past few months. I think her true colours would have been revealed by now. Dad loves her. He hasn't come right out and said it yet, but you can see it in his eyes. The way he's captivated by every word she says. She doesn't talk down to him. She treats him like an equal. To me, that says a lot. In fact, I haven't seen anything that I would class as detrimental in their relationship at all, and believe me, I'm sure something would have cropped up by now."

"Why have you spent so much time with them?" Lesley asked, her tone full of bitterness.

"Because I was willing to give her a chance, if only for Dad's sake. You not reaching out, not giving them a chance, is only punishing Dad. He's bound to want to keep his distance if you're giving off negative vibes."

"He has a short memory. After Mum died, I moved back home for a month or so, to ensure he got over her death."

"And he appreciated that. You keeping your distance from him now is, frankly, cutting him to shreds. I can tell, even if he hasn't come right out and said it."

After another deathly silence, Lesley muttered, "I don't know where to start. It's too late."

Sara smiled. "It's never too late, love. I'll tell you what, Mark and I will cook Sunday dinner this week. I'll ask Dad and Margaret along and help you break the ice with them. How does that sound?"

Another pause was then followed by a deep sigh. "I guess I'm up for it. I want to make amends, I hate being left out in the cold. You and Dad mean everything to me. I've missed you both."

"Honestly, we've missed you, too. But take it from me, if you cut Margaret out of your plans, then Dad is going to kick up such a fuss. She's a truly wonderful person, once you get to know her. She's done her very best to fit in with our family. Put yourself in her shoes for a moment or two. She's much older than us, very much set in her ways, and yet she's had to adapt to fit in with our needs as a family. I think the least we can do is ease the way for her, don't you?"

"I suppose you're right. I never really thought about it that way before. I feel a right bitch now. How can I make it up to her, to Dad?"

"Come along on Sunday with an open mind and heart. I'm telling you this once and once only, no one will ever replace Mum, not in my eyes nor in Dad's, but in Margaret, he's found a woman who cares deeply about him and his family. She's neat, not just in stature but as a person as well. Give her a chance, you won't regret it, I promise you."

"Okay, you've talked me around. Does she like flowers?"

"Tell me a woman who doesn't."

"Er... me."

Sara laughed and indicated into her road. "Okay, I'll give you that one. I'm home now. I'll catch up with you before Sunday, if I get the chance to. I've just taken on a brand-new murder case."

"Heck. Sorry, you could have done without me bending your ear on the way home. I know how much you like to unwind during the journey after a long day at work."

"Don't be silly. I'm always here for you, love. I'd hope you'd know that without me having to tell you all the time."

"I do. I'm sorry. I'll make it up to you."

"You don't have to. That's what sisters are for."

"Thanks for putting up with me, Sara, you're the best sister ever to have walked this earth."

"Hardly. See you on Sunday."

"You can count me in."

Sara smiled at the noticeable change in her sister's tone and ended the call.

Mark was standing on the doorstep, with Misty in his arms, to greet her.

"Sorry, I didn't get the chance to ring, I've had Lesley on the phone, trying to mend bridges."

Mark leaned in to kiss her and handed Misty over.

"Hey, you. Have you missed me?" She pecked her cat's face several times and then followed Mark into the house.

After removing her shoes and coat with one hand whilst holding Misty with the other, she entered the kitchen to find

Mark stirring the large pot on the stove. "I'm guessing we have curry tonight. The aroma is unmistakable."

"Correct. It's almost done now. Do you want to get changed? You have five minutes."

"Thanks. I won't be long. Dish up when it's ready." She placed Misty on the floor and darted out of the kitchen and upstairs where she changed into her burgundy velour suit. Then she bolted back down the stairs.

Mark had placed the plates on the table and was about to top up two glasses with red wine.

"God, I'm starving. Somehow, not sure how, Carla and I forgot to grab some lunch today."

"I must have known. I made enough to feed a small army. There's plenty more if you want it."

Sara stared down at the man-sized portion on her plate and laughed. "I think this will suffice. We could freeze the rest and have it next week."

"We'll see how much is left first. I bet you change your mind. Dig in. How has your day been? No, wait, you said you'd been on the phone to your sister. How is she? Still as stubborn as ever?"

Sara spooned a mouthful of rice and beef curry into her mouth and gestured for Mark to wait a moment. "Sorry, you caught me on the hop there. Lesley has admitted she's been in the wrong. I knew it wouldn't take her long before she felt left out. I've invited her round for dinner on Sunday. I'm hoping Dad and Margaret will join us."

"Suits me, as long as Lesley doesn't start again."

"She won't. Like I said, I believe that she's seen the error of her ways and is willing to give Margaret a go."

"Did she take much convincing?"

"This is delicious by the way. No, a few choice hard words from me appeared to do the trick."

"Your father has a right to be happy, even she has to recognise that fact."

"She does now, it's more or less what I told her. She's been pushed aside and has realised her mistake. Anyway, we'll soon find out on Sunday. I must give Dad a call later to arrange it. Hopefully he and Margaret haven't made other plans, like whizzing off in that mobile home of his. Actually, I'll do it now, it'll give my dinner a chance to cool down. I've already burnt the roof of my mouth."

Mark grinned, shook his head, and then continued with his meal.

"Hey, Dad, it's Sara. I haven't caught you at a bad time, have I? You sound out of breath."

Mark glanced up, and his eyes widened. Sara's cheeks heated up at the thought of what her father might have been up to.

"No, not at all. I was lugging things around the bedroom. I've been sorting through all your mother's personal paper-work, making sure I hadn't forgotten to tell anyone about her passing. It was Margaret's idea, she's so damned organised. Putting me to shame, she is."

"It must be a woman thing. Oops, saying that, Mark is the organised one in this house, not me."

"He's a good lad. I'm so proud of both of you. I never thought you'd settle down with another worthy man. Philip was in a class of his own, or so I thought, at the time. But Mark has proved me wrong over the years. You two are definitely the dream team."

Sara stared at the wonderful man in front of her, still tucking into his evening meal, and tears bulged. "I know just how lucky I am, Dad, believe me. We were wondering if you have any plans for Sunday."

"I don't think so. Margaret was talking about going out for a pub meal. Why, would you like to join us?"

"Not this time, maybe in the future. Umm… how about coming here instead? I have a surprise for you both."

"Ooo… in that case, how could we resist? The usual time, or do you want us there earlier?"

"How does twelve-thirty sound to you?"

"Perfect. Do you want us to bring anything?"

"No, just yourselves. Leave everything else to us. Enjoy the rest of your week, Dad."

"You, too, sweetheart. Love you."

"I love you, too." Sara ended the call and wiped away the tears threatening to fall.

"Hey, what's up?" Mark reached across the table for her hand.

She linked fingers with him. "Nothing. He reminded me of how lucky I am to have you, that's all."

Mark raised an eyebrow and squeezed her hand. "I'm the lucky one. If you hadn't brought Misty in that day, our paths might never have crossed, and we'd both still be miserable singletons."

"I suppose you're right."

"I take it they're coming on Sunday."

"Yep. I hope Dad hasn't done the wrong thing, accepting the invitation without discussing it with Margaret first."

"She'll be fine, you worry too much."

"Old habits die hard. This family has had a lot to contend with in the last three or four years."

"I know. Eat up before your dinner gets cold."

Sara smiled and nodded. She dipped her head before Mark got the chance to see further tears emerging. During the meal, they discussed what should be on the menu for the special family reunion.

"Why don't I buy a rib of beef for a change?"

"Sounds perfect to me, although I wouldn't know where to begin with cooking it."

He winked at her. "You leave the worrying to me, I'm a dab hand with beef in the kitchen."

"I'm sold. Want me to pick it up on the way home during the week?"

"Nope, I don't want any of that supermarket crap. A special occasion like this deserves the best meat to be served. I'll have a word with Clive the butcher, see what he can come up with between now and Saturday."

"I hope things turn out okay on the day. I'd hate all this effort we're about to put in to go to waste if Lesley goes against what she promised."

"Maybe give her a call in a couple of days to ensure she doesn't change her mind in the meantime."

"That's a good idea. What an absolute nightmare it is, juggling your family's feelings."

"Yeah, it's a bummer, but hey, life would be dull if we didn't have any drama to contend with, wouldn't it?"

"Too true. Now where was I with this delicious meal? Maybe it will be cool enough for me to eat without causing any further damage."

"Sorry, it's hot in flavour as well which isn't helping."

"I don't mind. You're a treasure for putting up with me, spoiling me on a daily basis."

"Ditto. There aren't many women who would put up with a messy male taking over their kitchen."

Sara's gaze drifted to the mess on the worktop. "No comment."

CHAPTER 4

First thing, Sara did the usual morning round with the staff, to see if there was any progress on the investigation. Disappointingly there wasn't, so she decided to venture out with Carla to see what Paul Hanson had to say for himself.

"Sorry, where are we going again, did you say?" Carla buckled up her seatbelt and asked.

"I thought I'd fill you in on the way." Sara pulled out of the station car park and onto the main road where the traffic had died down slightly compared to when she had arrived thirty minutes before.

"I'm listening."

She ran through the conversation she'd had with Lorraine the previous evening.

"What the hell? Why didn't she tell you sooner? Why the delay? You suspected there was something going on, didn't you?"

"Yep. That's why I decided to stop off at the mortuary on the way home last night, to try and get her to open up to me.

I never dreamed she would come out with something as bad as this."

"Surely, if he's threatened her, shouldn't we have come out here with backup to hand?"

"No. My take is that the man is grieving. If we show up mob-handed then it's only going to get his back up, isn't it?"

"I suppose. I wondered why you signed your Taser out this morning."

"I'm not that stupid, even if I give the impression I am now and again."

"That's debatable."

Sara jabbed her in the thigh. "Cheeky shit. So, when we get there, we go in with a compassionate heart, okay?"

"A compassionate heart, eh? That'll be a novelty."

"You know what I mean. I shouldn't have to spell it out to you. We should treat everyone the same until something bad rears its ugly head."

"And what if it's too late by then?"

"It won't be. Trust me."

Carla mumbled something that Sara couldn't quite catch, but she didn't bother asking her to repeat it.

"Here it is. Now remember what I said."

"Yes, yes, my compassionate heart is on full alert, don't worry."

"You can be such a sarcastic cow at times."

"Yeah, but having me as a partner brightens the dullest of days, doesn't it?"

"I'm yet to be convinced."

"Charming. I'll stay in the car and let you see to this psycho yourself then."

"Whatever," Sara called her bluff. She exited the car and walked towards the front door of the terraced house. It was neatly presented with window boxes and a hanging basket to the left of the front door displaying spring flowering bulbs and moss.

Carla caught up with her at the front door. Sara rang the bell.

The door opened, and a scruffy-looking man in his early thirties stood there, eyeing them cautiously.

"DI Sara Ramsey and DS Carla Jameson, Mr Hanson. Would it be all right if we come in and speak with you for a moment?"

"No. Have you got a warrant?"

"We haven't. I'll get one if you insist."

"What do you want?" He tucked most of his frame behind the door and gripped it with both hands above his head.

"We'd like to ask you a few questions, if you don't mind."

"Get to the point, about what?"

"About your reaction to your mother's death," Sara stated, still skirting around the truth.

"What are you talking about? My mother died, and I've been mourning her loss. I didn't realise there was a law against that; maybe I was wrong about that. It wouldn't surprise me nowadays, we're living in a nanny state after all."

"I don't think that's the case at all, sir. Okay, if you won't let us in to discuss your behaviour, I'm going to have to ask you to accompany us to the station for questioning."

He jumped out from behind the door and glared at them. "You what? You can't come knocking on my door and order me down to the station. I have rights, you know."

"We're well aware of your rights. There has been a serious allegation made against you that could be cleared up in an instant." The more Sara spoke to the man, the more incensed she was becoming. It was all well and good her telling Carla to be compassionate when dealing with this individual, but something in Sara's gut was waving a red flag, instructing her to be cautious. She hadn't come across anything like this before, not with someone she'd only just laid eyes on.

"Clear it up here and now then. Tell me what I've done wrong."

"No, I must insist that you accompany us to the station, sir. If you refuse, I will have no hesitation in arresting you."

"Umm... I think you'll find you can't do that without a reason."

He was right, but Sara wasn't about to let it go there. "Actually, threatening a member of the Home Office Pathology Lab is a criminal offence."

"I didn't. Not in so many words. I've lost my mother, my emotions were, and are, all over the place, and here you are, coming down heavy on me for overstepping the mark slightly."

Fed up with arguing the toss with him, Sara asked, "Will you accompany us to the station or not?"

He shrugged. "If it will get you off my damn back, then yes, all right."

"Good, we'll wait for you in the car."

He closed the door without answering.

"Unusual for you to ask someone to accompany us to the station," Carla mumbled on their way back to the car.

"I'm going with my gut on this one, there's something off about him. I might be doing him an injustice, what with him going through the grieving process, but..."

"I get you."

"Do you feel it, too?" Sara leaned against her car, her gaze drifting back to the house.

"I'm not sure if I'd go that far, but there's definitely something off about him."

"A good grilling down at the station should sort him out, I hope."

"We'll see. Here he is now. Is he coming in our car?"

"I'll get him to follow us," Sara confirmed.

However, Paul Hanson had other ideas. "You're going to need to drop me off again after you've finished with me."

"Can't you come in your car?"

"I would, if I had it. It's in the garage, no idea what's wrong with it. No doubt the mechanic will find a multitude of things wrong with it before he hands it back to me. It's been running like shit lately."

"Sorry to hear that. Okay, get in, we can arrange a lift back for you later. We shouldn't keep you too long."

He jumped into the back seat, apparently without a care in the world. During the journey, Sara kept a watchful eye on him through her rear-view mirror. A couple of times their gazes met, and she quickly turned her attention back to the road.

Pulling into her usual spot, she said, "Right, here we are."

"I've never been to a police station before, should I be worried?" he asked with a glint in his eye.

Sara got out of the car and opened the rear door for him. She smiled and replied, "It really depends if you have anything to hide or not."

Their gazes met once more, and he shook his head.

"I haven't. Do I get fed and watered here?"

"We can arrange to bring you a tea or coffee during the interview. No food, I'm afraid. Like I said, you probably won't be here long anyway."

"What you're really saying is this is all going to be a time-wasting exercise, right?"

"I'm hoping that won't be the case, only time will tell. Follow me please, Mr Hanson."

"If I have to."

They entered the reception area, and Jeff, the desk sergeant, cocked an inquisitive eyebrow.

"Is there an interview room available, Jeff? Sorry, I should have rung ahead and booked one."

"You're in luck, ma'am, we've got one available."

"Can you do the necessary for me?"

"I'll get an officer to join you in a moment. Any drinks required?"

"Mr Hanson?" Sara asked.

"Coffee, no sugar, white, thanks."

"And Carla and I will have our usual, thanks, Jeff."

"Interview Room Two. I'll put your request in and bring them through, ma'am."

Sara smiled and covered the number pad to insert her code and then made her way down the long corridor to the room at the bottom with Hanson sandwiched between her and Carla.

"Cleaner than I thought it would be," Hanson noted, smirking.

"We do our best." Sara opened the door and instructed Hanson to take a seat on the nearside of the table.

They were joined seconds later by a uniformed male officer.

Carla said the necessary verbiage for the recording machine, and Sara got the interview underway.

"Mr Hanson, I appreciate how raw things must be for you right now, but perhaps you wouldn't mind going over the incident that led to your mother's death."

His brow pinched into deep lines. "I don't understand."

"What part don't you understand, sir?"

"You know damn well what happened to my mother, so why question me about it? Causing me even more angst."

"I need to make sure I have the facts right. So, if you wouldn't mind."

He heaved out a breath. There was a knock on the door, and a female officer entered and deposited three cups on the table and then left the room. Hanson wrapped his hands around his plastic cup and stared at the contents for a while.

"Mr Hanson, or would it be all right if I called you Paul?"

"Whatever suits you, I answer to both names and a few more." He glanced up and grinned.

"Fine. Paul, for the recording, I'd like you to run through what happened the day your mother died."

"She was disabled; I've been her carer for years. She had a turn, hadn't been right all day. She was in bed most of the day. I gave her lunch as usual, we had pasta then I checked in on her to see if she wanted anything for tea. She wanted a sandwich, which I made for her. I left her eating it along with a cup of tea and then went to collect her plate later and found her struggling to breathe. She told me she was dying, so I called for an ambulance. They took bloody hours to arrive."

He stopped talking and turned his cup in his hands.

"Go on. What did the paramedics say?"

"They thought she'd had a heart attack. They transferred her to the back of the ambulance, were taking her to hospital when... she died. They tried to revive her, but there was nothing, no response from her. If they had showed up sooner, she would have got through this. Her heart was in good condition. She's always been a strong woman."

"And yet she was disabled. What sort of disability did she have?"

"A degenerative wasting disease that attacked her nervous system. The doctors are still trying to work out what it is, they've been trying to figure it out for years. Bloody hopeless gobs of shite, they are. Once a family member takes on the responsibility of being a carer, that's it, they couldn't give a shit. They regard that person out of the system; at least that's how it seems."

"I'm sorry you feel that way. I'm sure if you reached out

for help that some sort of assistance would be available to you."

"We had a carer come in for a few hours a week. We had to pay for her visits, though. Mum got Attendance Allowance, and it came out of that, so no big deal."

"So the carer coming in gave you the respite you needed, did she?"

"Not really. She was there for a couple of hours… when she turned up, all it did was allow me to get on top of the other chores I didn't have the time to deal with normally, so no rest for the wicked, as they say."

"That's a shame. I should imagine that caring full-time is a thankless task most days."

He looked up and nodded. "Yes, most days. But I loved my mother and wanted the best for her. We couldn't afford to put her in a home. Do you know how much money they wanted per month? Four grand! Who the fuck has that sort of dosh lying around? Bloody Tories, they've ruined this country."

"Ouch, that is a lot of money. What about your mother's house, could you not have sold that and paid for her care?"

"That would have only lasted so long. What would have happened after the money ran out? I would have needed to have found her somewhere else to live. Anyway, I lived with Mum, so if I'd sold the house, I would have been making myself homeless at the same time."

"The proverbial catch-twenty-two situation then," Sara said.

"Yes. That's right. No easy solution at all. Still, I don't have to worry about that now… that she's gone."

His demeanour altered, and his gaze dropped to his cup once more.

"I understand how upsetting all this must be for you,

however, I have to ask why you felt the need to threaten the pathologist working on your mother's case?"

"I didn't."

"That's not my understanding at all. The pathologist and her team are there to help us solve crimes, you're aware of that, aren't you?"

He glanced up, and his eyes narrowed. "I'm not stupid. Why?"

"It's just that when the pathologist carried out the post-mortem she found no reason for your mother to have a heart attack."

"What are you saying? That she didn't have one?" He scratched the side of his head and then slipped his hands back around his cup.

"No, she had one, okay, but the pathologist carried out further tests to gain a better insight into her death and was surprised to learn…" Sara paused to gauge his reaction.

"What? Are you expecting me to fill in the blanks for you? I can't because I don't have a bloody clue what you're on about."

"It would appear that your mother had been poisoned."

He flung himself back in his chair, and his mouth dropped open. He bounced forward again. "What?" He pointed at Sara. "I can tell where this is leading, and I'm telling you now, you're wrong. I didn't poison her. I loved my mother, she was all I had. Yes, I've struggled over the years but had slotted into a routine. Life was okay, it wasn't perfect, not by a long shot, but we coped. I coped. How the heck would I poison her? I wouldn't know where to begin. It wasn't me, I'm telling you. Why won't you believe me?"

Sara raised a hand. "You were her full-time carer, she had little to no contact with the outside world."

He waved a finger. "You're wrong. Someone came in, I've already told you that."

"Where from, an agency?"

"Yes, that's right. Carers Today, they're a local company, I've been using them for the past year or so."

"And only one woman showed up regularly, or did several different women tend to your mother?"

"No, just the one. Tina Sawyer is her name. Yes, she's done this. She hates me. She's trying to lay the blame at my door because I cared for Mum full-time. What the fuck? You have to believe me, she's the one who poisoned my mother, not me."

"How do you know that? Do you have any proof that's the case?"

"No… yes, wait. There was that incident with Mum's purse last month."

"What incident?"

"I walked into the room to find Tina taking money out of Mum's purse. I pulled Tina up about it. She denied it, of course, but I know what I saw."

Sara inclined her head, perturbed by his suggestion. "Did you complain to the agency?"

"No, I didn't want the hassle, and Mum liked her, not sure why, but Mum always responded well to her when she was there. I decided to let things lie. Don't tell me I've done the wrong thing and this woman was poisoning her all along?" He placed his hands over his face and sobbed.

Sara and Carla exchanged uncertain glances.

"Try not to upset yourself too much. I'm sorry but I have to ask these questions."

"I get that. But you have to believe me when I tell you I had nothing to do with this."

"Okay, don't worry. I assure you, we will get to the bottom of this. Is there anything else you can tell me about this woman?"

"She's called Tina Sawyer, she's from the local council estate. That should be enough, shouldn't it?"

Sara raised an eyebrow. "Are you under the impression that everyone living on a council estate has a dubious past?"

"If the cap fits, then yes."

"That's not something you should be banding around, sir. You need to take everyone's different circumstances into consideration, you shouldn't tar everyone with the same brush."

"You do what you do and I'll do what I do, especially after my experience with this foul-mouthed, angry woman."

"Angry? Did she show signs of anger towards your mother whilst she cared for her?"

"Not as such. But stealing from an old woman's purse, for fuck's sake, that's pretty low, wouldn't you agree?"

"Maybe. If that's what happened."

His eyes narrowed and peered into her soul.

"Okay, let's go back to the threats you made towards the pathologist, shall we?"

"You can do what you like." He sat back and folded his arms over his heaving chest. "You'd be pretty miffed if the pathologist tried to stop you from paying your final respects to your mother."

"There are ways you can do that without barging your way into the mortuary storage area. Which I am led to believe is what occurred. Is that correct?"

"If you say so. That woman stood in my way. She seemed to be enjoying my discomfort, so I tore past her to try and find my mother. Why can't people in authority show a little compassion when dealing with loved ones?"

"As far as I'm aware, the pathologist in question is one of the most compassionate people in her field."

"Is that right? Well, she lacked any when dealing with me. Everything seemed an effort, even talking to me."

"I'm sorry you felt that way, however, it didn't give you the right to threaten her."

"I didn't, not really. The trouble with your lot is you always stick together and come down heavily on guys like me. I'm going through the grieving process; obviously that doesn't count for anything in your eyes, does it? Shame on you. All of you. Are we done here? Because I think we are. That's all I'm prepared to say, and as this interview was voluntary, I think we should end it here."

"If that's what you want. I'm sorry you think I came down heavily on you. I do understand that you're grieving. I apologise if I've caused any offence. That wasn't my intention. All I'm searching for is the truth."

"And I've given it to you. You need to track down this Tina Sawyer and have a word with her."

"Thank you. We'll do that today. I'll make arrangements for you to get a lift home."

"Thanks." He sat back again and stared at the wall behind Sara.

Sara gestured for Carla to complete the interview, and then they both left the room.

"Jeff, can you arrange to drop Mr Hanson off at home for me?" Sara said.

"Of course I can. Leave it with me, ma'am."

Sara and Carla made their way back upstairs.

"I take it we're going to question Tina Sawyer next?" Carla asked.

They reached the top of the stairs, and Sara turned to watch Paul Hanson go back into the reception area with the uniformed officer.

"Yep, I'm not convinced about his tale, but we're going to have to chase it up all the same."

"I'll get onto the agency and see if they can give me her details."

"Right. I'll see if the rest of the team has anything new for us on the other investigation."

"We've definitely got our hands full."

"We have. It makes life interesting, doesn't it?"

Carla was the closest to the door. She entered the incident room first, and Sara followed her.

After Sara had completed her chore, she returned to Carla's desk. "Anything?"

"Yep, after a while they gave me her address. Told me she was working the early shift today and would be finished at twelve."

"Okay, it's eleven-thirty now, we might as well head over there, see if we can catch her in. We'll pick up some lunch on the way to make up for the one we missed out on yesterday."

"I'd forgotten all about that, no wonder I was ravenous when I got home."

"Me, too."

THEY SET off and stopped at a local café to have a bacon sandwich and coffee, then got on the road again at ten minutes past twelve.

"That's a great way to waste time." Carla smiled and rubbed her stomach.

"It's good to have an occasional splurge."

Sara drew up outside a terraced house in the middle of the council estate and scanned the area. Not a single house seemed to be cared for by its tenants. "Appalling. I blame the landlord. The council don't give a shit about estates like this."

"Yeah, they used to, but not these days. Some of these houses are falling into disrepair." Carla pointed at the house across the green from them.

Sara shuddered. "Disgusting. Still, there's not a lot we can do to alter the situation, as much as we'd like to."

"We could put a complaint in, for what good it will do the tenants."

"Remind me to do it when we get back."

"Really?"

"What harm can it do? No one should be forced to live in tips like these, should they?"

"You're right."

"Back to business. I think we've been spotted."

A woman was standing at the window of the house in front of them, just staring out at the street, in a daze. They exited the car.

"She's leaving her viewing point and going to the front door," Carla replied.

"You reckon? Maybe she's doing a runner and heading out the back instead."

"Nah, I'm right. Here she is now."

Sara produced her ID and held it up. "Tina Sawyer?"

"That's right. I've been expecting you. The agency told me you'd made an enquiry. They didn't tell me what this was about, though. Do you want to come in?"

"Thanks."

Tina stood behind the door and allowed them to enter. "Come through to the lounge. Can I get you a drink?"

"No, we're fine. Have you been at work today?"

"Yes, I'm not in a habit of wearing my uniform when I'm off-duty. I have to nip back out later to put an old man to bed, so it's not worth changing. Take a seat."

Tina sat in the armchair closest to the gas fire which was on low and gestured for Sara and Carla to sit on the sofa which had tatty, threadbare arms.

"What did you need to see me about?"

"One of your clients, a Mrs Hanson."

Tina shook her head. "I was so sad to hear that she had

died. She was getting worse every time I visited her, although it still came as a shock to hear the news."

"You visited regularly then?"

"Yes, once or twice a week to give Paul a break, not that he went out while I was there. He always milled around in the background. You know, as if he didn't trust me."

"We've had a word with him down at the station this morning, and he mentioned having a problem with you. Do you know what I'm getting at?"

Her gaze instantly plummeted to the floor. "I think so. Was it about the money?"

"It was. Care to fill us in?"

Her head rose, and she looked Sara in the eye. "I told him he'd got it all wrong, but he refused to listen to me."

"What happened?"

"I was talking to Pauline, his mum, about a fix I was in. She was such a sweet lady, she told me to take thirty pounds out of her purse to help me out. At first, I refused, but she insisted, said it was no use to her and that it was just sitting there. My heart was filled with love for that woman. I know there are all these videos doing the rounds about carers stealing from their clients, but I would never dream of doing that. I promised Pauline that I would pay the money back the next week and that's what I did. Paul, well, he treated me like a common thief. Wouldn't listen to what I had to say. Pauline tried her very best to speak up for me, but he was having none of it. He made my life hell for a week."

"In what way?"

"Giving me the cold shoulder, looking daggers at me every time I entered the room, that sort of thing. Once my wages were paid into my bank, I withdrew the thirty quid and gave it back to Pauline as promised. She never had any doubts about my honesty. It was a one-off. I'd had extra expenses to fork out the previous month, a large vet's bill to pay because my cat was ill. As you can imagine, I'm on a tight budget, my wages are crap, and with the energy bills going through the roof, my budgeting skills are non-existent at the moment."

"As is half the country, I shouldn't wonder. Paul knew that you had repaid the money?"

"Yes, I told him, and his mother confirmed it. He grunted and walked out of the room. I was mortified to sink to that level, but Pauline was a lovely lady. She knew me, knew that I was an honest person and offered to help me out. If I hadn't paid my landlord the rent money that week, he said he was going to evict me."

"Aren't these properties council owned?" Sara asked, confused.

"They used to be, not these days, no. My landlord owns virtually all the houses on this estate. They're all in need of repair, and the council refuses to do a damn thing about it. It's as if Smith, my landlord, has them in his back pocket. I hate living here, but the rent is cheap, I couldn't possibly afford to live somewhere else, not on my crappy wages, and I love my job, so they've got me by the short and curlies, all of them."

"I'm sorry, that's a terrible situation to be in."

"Hey, I'm okay most of the time. Save your sympathy for those who have recently been forced to leave their properties around here because of the cost-of-living crisis. I know at least four people who now have their names on cardboard boxes down by the river. What a bloody state this country has become, and all you ever hear on the TV is this country needs your help, there's been a disaster, er... newsflash, there are people in the UK who are dying, who have died over the winter because they couldn't afford to heat their homes. Who dipped their hands into their pockets to save those people? No one, that's who. Proud people, they are, who refuse to ask for help. Okay, sorry about that, it needed to be said, if only to get it out of my system."

"I agree. It's a shocking state of affairs, and someone has to be made to pay for causing people so much misery in this country. Anyway, going back to you returning the money, how did Paul react to the news?"

"Indifferently, I suppose you'd say. He still treated me like I was dirt on the bottom of his shoes. Never had a conversation with me. When I asked him how Pauline had been when I showed up at work, he shrugged and told me to ask her myself."

Sara studied the woman's disposition as she was talking. "Are you all right, Tina?"

"No, not really. I'm gutted Pauline has gone. She was such a beautiful person, inside and out. We had a rapport that I don't have with my other clients. Yes, she was one in a million all right. I'm going to miss her, and before you say it, not only because she got me out of a fix either. She'd become my friend since I started caring for her. I'm puzzled as to why she died. She seemed pretty healthy to me, apart from the disability. The agency told me she'd had a heart attack. How is that even possible?"

Sara liked this woman, so she didn't see any reason to skirt around the truth. "A post-mortem was carried out on Pauline's body after she died, and the results were what we'd call interesting."

Tina stared at Sara and tilted her head. "What are you saying? That she didn't die of natural causes?"

Sara shook her head. "It would appear that she had been poisoned."

"What the f...? Sorry for my language. Are you winding me up?"

"Sadly not. When we interviewed her son earlier today, he appeared to be pointing the finger at you."

Tina shot out of her chair and crossed the room to look out of the window. "No way. What the bloody hell is he on about? I loved Pauline as if she was a member of my own family. I could never hurt her, *never*." She returned to her seat, her gaze fixed on Sara. "You have to believe me. Bloody hell, I wouldn't know where to bloody begin, poisoning someone. That's disgusting that Paul should put my name in the frame. Why would he do that?" She asked and then stared at the floor in front of her, then clicked her thumb and finger together. "Unless he did it and is trying to get you to think it's me. Jesus, the conniving little toerag."

"Either way, that's why we're here, to question you about the incident. Did you visit Pauline on the day she died?"

"No, the last time I visited her was two days before. I only went twice a week, once at the beginning of the week and the second visit was on a Friday. I can't believe he would tell you it was me. What a scumbag he is. Was she poisoned in one go or over time?"

"We're not sure yet, further tests are being carried out by the pathologist as we speak. We won't let the matter drop until we've found out the truth."

"I should think not. But I'm telling you this, you won't find the answers you seek here. Why would I poison her? What would I have to gain from her death? He used to get frustrated with her all the time. I never saw him as the doting son type at all. Please, you have to believe me, this isn't me just laying the blame at someone else's door, this is me speaking the truth. I've been in this game for nearly thirty years, living hand to mouth most days, but I wouldn't change a thing. This job isn't just a job to most of us, it's a vocation, caring for people who desperately need us."

"Please, don't go upsetting yourself. I'm sure you can see this from our point of view. We have to question you since a serious crime has been committed."

Tears fell. "I do. But you have to believe me," she pleaded. "I had nothing to do with this. You're barking up the wrong tree. Look around, search my home for any evidence. Yes, I'm giving you the permission you need to carry out an in-depth search because I haven't done anything wrong. I swear to you I haven't." She pulled a tissue out of the pocket in the front of her bag and blew her nose.

"All right. I believe you. Do you know if any other people visited Pauline at all?"

"No, only me. They had no other family in the area, and all of Pauline's friends had abandoned her once her illness struck."

"That's very sad. So Paul was forced to look after her, is that what you're telling us?"

"Yes. There were days when he treated her nicely and others when he treated her abysmally, but I had to keep my mouth shut, otherwise he would have asked the agency to have sent someone else in my place."

"Why didn't he do that after the money incident?"

She shrugged and mulled over the question. "I'm not sure. Unless… he planned all of this."

"Planned what? Killing his mother and setting you up to take the fall for her death?"

"Yes. You have no idea how manipulative he can be. I've seen it with my own eyes."

"Have you ever seen him ill-treat his mother?"

"Not directly, no, but I've visited her, and she's had bruises on her arms and face before. When I asked her how she got them, she refused to answer. Actually, that's a fib, she told me that she fell. There's no way she was telling me the truth, the bruises were in places you wouldn't pick up if you fell. In this job, you get to know these things."

"So you've suspected that Paul has been hurting his

mother for a while then? Did you mention it to anyone at the agency?"

"No. I was tempted to, but you know what it's like yourself when you have little to no evidence to hand to back up your theories. It's all such a mess, now that she's gone. Do you think he would have it in him to kill his own mother?"

Sara chewed her lip and shrugged again. "I'm beginning to wonder. Will you give us a statement?"

"Of course. I'll help all I can if you think it will bring him to justice. If he did kill her then you need to throw the book at him. She was such a sweet, endearing woman."

"Don't worry, we will, with your help."

"You can count on me. He needs to be stopped. If that man can kill his own mother, you have to wonder what else he is capable of."

"Exactly. Okay, we're going to head back over to his house and have another chat with him. I'll see if a uniformed officer can drop by today and get a statement from you. If that's not possible, they'll give you a ring to see when it's convenient to pay you a visit. Can you give me your number?"

Sara jotted down the number, and she and Carla left the house.

"Well, that was a bit of an eye-opener. Things escalated quickly, too. Are you sure about this, Sara?"

"Aren't you? Why do you think I wanted to interview him at the station? Something didn't sit right with me. If he's the killer, then that's why."

"Jesus… who in their right mind would bloody kill their own mother?"

"To be fair, it must be hard caring for someone day in, day out, giving up the life you once had to be at their beck and call twenty-four-seven. Not that I'm making excuses for him. But let's cut him some slack all the same. If he poisoned her, then perhaps he thought that would be a fitting way out of the situation for both of them."

"Instead of choosing to smother her with a pillow, you mean?"

"Yep. Either way, I think we should head back over there and invite him back to the station and interview him under caution this time."

"Alone?"

"Yes, alone. What's up with you always wanting backup to accompany us lately?"

"I wasn't aware that was the case. All I'm doing is just double-checking with you. Pardon me for breathing."

"Behave yourself and get in the car."

CHAPTER 5

*S*ara knocked on Hanson's door, but it remained unanswered. She kicked herself for being slack and letting him go when there was a stream of doubts running through her mind. "Shit, shit, shit!"

"And some," Carla mumbled. "What now?"

"Now we put out an alert for his car."

"Good luck with that one, he could be bloody miles away by now."

Sara's eyes widened. "All right, there's no need to rub it in. I screwed up, I don't need reminding of that fact, okay?"

Carla bowed her head in shame. "Sorry, you know I'm guilty of letting my mouth run away from me at times."

"Fortunately, it doesn't happen that often. If it did, you would no longer be my partner. My job is hard enough as it is without someone taking pride in pointing out my mistakes."

"Hey, that's a tad over the top."

"Excuse me," a female voice said from the side.

Sara pinned a smile in place. "Yes, can I help?"

"I was wondering if you were after Paul. I saw you here earlier, didn't I?"

Sara flashed her warrant card. "Yes, we're police officers. Have you seen him?"

"He left about half an hour ago."

Damn! We've missed our opportunity now! "Did he say where he was going?"

"Away for a while, he told me. The size of the bag he was carrying, I'd say at least a couple of weeks. You know what men are like, they prefer to travel light."

"And he didn't mention where he was going or when he would be back?"

The neighbour paused to think. "No. I did think it was strange, you know, for him to go gallivanting with his mother's funeral to plan; well, you would, wouldn't you? He told me everything was in hand and he needed to get away."

"Does he have any relatives or friends living close by?"

"No family. He and his mother didn't have any relatives, not living around here. As for friends, he doesn't really seem the type to have any. I could be wrong, though."

"Did he take off in his own car?"

"Yes, that's right. Has he done something wrong? Been up to no good?"

"Not really. We're investigating his mother's death, and some queries have arisen that we need to run past him. They'll keep, for now. Thanks so much for your help."

"My pleasure. He's a weird one, that boy. Needs to learn some manners while he's away. Snapped at me for being concerned about him when I heard that his mother had died. There was no call for it, none whatsoever. You try and do your best for people when a loved one has passed away... well, I won't be doing that again in a hurry, I can tell you."

"I'm sorry he treated you badly. Have you lived next door to them long?"

"Yes, around five years. I used to be in there all the time, helping out with Pauline before she got really bad. One day, out of the blue, he told me his mother said she didn't want to see me any more. I was gobsmacked, I was. We always got on great, Pauline and me. I sent a few meals next door and a few gifts, or tried to, you know, to cheer her up. I always found them sitting on my doorstep the following morning with a note written on them. 'Stick your gifts', signed by Pauline. There's no way she would have been as rude as that. I knew it had to be him. There was no getting past him. As much as I wanted to reach out to Pauline, he was always there, standing in the way."

"In other words, he was determined to cut her off from her friends?"

The woman in her sixties pointed a wrinkled finger. "That's what I thought. That's why I didn't give up, not for a few months. In the end, I thought to myself, what's the bloody point? I have other people I can be of service to, friends, neighbours and family who are keen on my help. You know when you're banging your head against a brick wall, don't you?"

"I'm sorry they treated you that way, throwing your kind gestures back in your face," Sara replied.

"Ha! Not them, *him*, it was all down to him. Earlier, I asked if there was anything I could do to help with the funeral arrangements. The bugger gave me the finger and told me to keep my effing nose out. I don't deserve to be treated like that, not when all I'm trying to do is bloody help. Still, that's it now, I've been more than fair with him, he can go whistle for all I care. If he prefers to be all alone, then that's up to him, let him get on with it, I say. I'm through with showing him any form of kindness only for it to be thrown back in my face."

"I don't blame you either. There are some people in this

world you just can't help. If I leave you my card, will you give me a call if, or when, he shows up again?"

"Of course I will, it goes without saying. He's a very foolish man, cutting people off like this, when he's likely to need our help. His mother deserved so much more. I doubt if he will give her a good sendoff. None of us have been informed when the funeral is going to take place, none of us. Some of the other neighbours have asked me if I know, but I don't. We'd all like to pay our respects to the woman on the day, but he has other ideas. Do you know if there is a way around it? Can we attend the funeral even if he doesn't want us there?"

"I believe anyone can attend a funeral but maybe it would be better manners to ask. Maybe when he returns, he'll be in a better frame of mind to deal with it. I wouldn't badger him, just drop a few hints when he gets back. It's nice that you thought a lot of Mrs Hanson."

"She was a dear soul. I wish I could have done more for her while she was alive. I'm telling you, if it hadn't been for his attitude, she would have been cared for by most of us in this community. Why would someone turn their back on people willing to lend a hand? It's a thankless task, caring for a loved one, day in and day out, I should know, I did it with my mother a few years ago. That's why I was keen to help."

"You're a thoughtful person. I'm sorry he misunderstood your kindness for what it was. Try not to take it to heart. I think he's a very confused young man at present."

"Even more reason to reach out to people for help, but hey, who am I to question what he gets up to?" She tapped Sara's card in her hand. "I'll ring you when he shows up."

"Hopefully, that won't be long. Maybe the time away will make him come to his senses."

The neighbour rolled her eyes. "You reckon? I doubt it very much."

Sara smiled and turned back towards the car. "Shit! We need to find him before he gets very far."

"I'll get onto Jill, see if she can find out what car he has and get an alert put out on him," Carla stated. She removed her phone from her pocket and got on with the task.

Sara entered the car in a daze. *How has it come to this? Why didn't I arrest him at the station? Because he duped me, played me for a fool and wrapped me around his little finger.*

"Hey, what's going on in that head of yours?" Carla asked. She was still on the phone to the station.

"I can't get past the feeling that's eating away at me, that I've somehow screwed up."

"You haven't. I was with you all the way on this one, Sara, stop crucifying yourself. He had us both fooled. Anyway, this is an extra case we're dealing with, our priorities should still lie with the murder inquiry."

"I agree with you, however, if Paul Hanson poisoned his mother, then this case is also a murder inquiry and shouldn't be ignored."

"Fair point. Jesus, why do we always take on these cases when we're snowed under with work all the time? We never seem to catch a break in between cases, do we?"

"We're doing Lorraine a favour, one of our own."

"I know, I didn't mean it to sound selfish. I'll shut up."

"I should. I'm trying to think."

"Hi, Jill, yeah, I'm still here." Carla put the phone on speaker now that they were sitting in the car.

"I've got his reg, make and model of the car. It's a black Honda Accord."

She added the registration number, and Sara scribbled it in her notebook.

"Thanks, Jill. I want an alert out for the car. You've got his address, see if the boys can pick his reg up on any CCTV or ANPRs in the area. Do we know where he works?"

Carla shook her head. "He was a full-time carer for his mother, or had you forgotten that?"

"Momentarily, yes. Shit! He has no family or friends in the area and he's on the bloody run. Where the heck is he likely to turn up?" Sara smacked her hand on the steering wheel several times.

Carla said nothing but wagged her finger at her.

Sara inhaled a breath that she hoped would steady her racing heart. "Okay, we're heading back to base."

"All right, boss. See you soon."

Carla ended the call and let out several expletives of her own. "What the fuck do we do now? What if the cameras don't pick him up? Or the alert fails?"

"I wish I knew," Sara replied. She switched on the engine and revved the throttle a few times which made her feel slightly better. "We had him in our grasp... I feel such a prat for letting him go."

"I know that feeling. We can't dwell on it, it's going to eat away at us even more. We have to push this out of our mind and concentrate on the case we were dealing with."

"I know you're right, but having two killers on the loose out there is only going to make me feel ten times worse than I do now. I'm at fault. We'd better get back. The first thing I'm going to need upon our return is to enter the confessional box with the DCI."

"Ouch, rather you than me. She'll be fine, these things happen to less professional inspectors than you, Sara. I repeat, stop being so hard on yourself."

"I know. But the fact that I've let Lorraine down keeps going round and round in my head. She's having a really tough time at the moment over this shit. Once I tell her that I had him within my grasp and let him go... she's going to nail me to the frigging wall and slice me to pieces with that scalpel of hers."

Carla laughed. "As if."

"I'm glad you find my prickly predicament amusing."

"I don't, not in that sense. It's your overreaction that is killing me. Lorraine will be fine, you mark my words. Nothing I say will make you feel better so I'm going to give up trying, how's that?"

"Thanks, partner, I knew I could count on you for support."

Carla grinned.

As it was, the rest of the day proved fruitless except for one small matter. Craig and Barry had spotted Hanson's car heading out of the city. The time on the ANPR showed that he'd taken off the second Tina Sawyer had opened her front door to Sara and Carla.

"He didn't hang around getting out of town, did he?" Sara mumbled, more to herself than anyone on her team.

She punched herself in the thigh and immediately caught Carla shaking her head. She mouthed an apology, and her partner accepted it.

"Okay, I'm calling it a day. It's gone seven now. We haven't found another sighting of him yet. The ANPRs will be doing their job throughout the evening, so there's no reason for us to stick around any longer, agreed?"

They all nodded, and most of them seemed defeated by the day's miserable outcome.

"Guys, don't take this home with you. We've done our best. We're stretched at this moment, working the two cases, so as my good partner over here is fond of saying, 'Don't beat yourself up over this'. I'm sure it'll come right in the end. Let's remain positive at all times. Negativity is never good for the soul, remember that. Now go home and get some rest, and we'll pick up where we left off in the morning."

Sara perched on the desk by the door and smiled and said farewell to each of them as they passed.

"Enjoy the rest of your evening, boss," Jill replied, the slightest of smiles touching her lips.

Sara reached out and laid a hand on her forearm. "You, too, love. Chin up. We'll get the bastard."

Carla remained behind with Sara. The first words out of her mouth were, "I hope you're going to listen to your own advice."

Sara smiled. "Yep, I'm not going to give this case another thought for the rest of the evening."

Inclining her head, Carla tutted. "Yeah, I'll believe that when I see it. I mean it, you need to let it go this evening. Have a good night's sleep, and we'll hit the investigation and any possible leads that come in overnight hard first thing. Come on, we should both call it a day. I know I'm knackered, physically and mentally."

"You go on ahead. I want to make a final call first and then, I promise, I'll get on the road."

"You can ring Lorraine en route," Carla said with a smirk.

"You think you can read me like a book, don't ya?"

"Yep." Carla snatched her bag off the back of her seat and headed towards the door. "Send her my regards. See you in the morning. Oh, and be careful what you tell her."

"I will. See you."

Sara gave in, switched off the rest of the lights in the office and headed out of the door. In the car, she dialled Lorraine's mobile. It went to voicemail, so she left a message. "Hi, just checking in on you. Give me a call if you can later."

She ended the call and settled into her drive home, listening to her favourite love song compilation. Ten minutes from home, she rang Mark. "I won't be long. Do you need anything?"

"Nope, wait, yes."

Sara's heart sank at the thought of having to turn around and go back to the supermarket. "What's that?"

He said one word in the sexiest voice he possessed, "You."

She laughed out loud. "Anytime you like, Mr Fisher."

"As I thought, Mrs Fisher-Ramsey."

She laughed again. They had agreed when they had tied the knot three years before that she wouldn't change her name at work, it was more complicated when you were in the Force. "I'll be with you in ten minutes. What's on the menu tonight?"

"I thought we'd already established that," came her husband's swift retort.

"You're incorrigible. Love you."

"Love you more."

She hung up, her thoughts returning to their ongoing investigations. "I hope to God we find something soon that will help solve both cases. It's going to stretch our resources to the limit otherwise."

As usual, her devoted husband was waiting for her on the doorstep with Misty in his arms. They shared a kiss, and he handed over Misty while he took her coat off.

"You can remove your shoes yourself, I'm not that agile these days."

"I wouldn't say that." She slipped off one of her heels and then the other and followed him into the kitchen. "So, what is for dinner?" She sniffed the air but failed to determine what was in the oven.

"Pork chop, veg and roast potatoes."

"Oh my, you do spoil me." Her mobile rang as she went to kiss him again. "It's probably Lorraine. I tried to call her from the car, asked her to ring me back when she could."

"It's fine. I have plenty to keep me busy here."

"I'll get changed while I speak to her." She headed back

into the hallway and up the stairs where she answered the call. "Hi, how are you?"

"Harassed. I got your call, was it anything urgent?"

"No, I was checking in on you, that's all. Why are you harassed?"

"The usual. I can't talk for long, there was a fatal accident earlier today. I've got another two PMs to get through before I can shut up shop for the night. It's been a full day, and the evening is going to be just as busy."

"Lorraine, you can't keep pushing yourself like this, girl. When are you going to give in and admit you need an extra pair of hands down there?"

"Probably when I'm on my knees, which could be sooner than either of us realises. I'm fine. What are you up to? Are you still at work?"

"No, I'm at home. Mark is cooking the dinner."

"Have I told you lately how envious I am of your setup?"

"Often. The offer still stands for you to come and stay with us."

"As much as I love you guys, you'd soon fall out with me turning up at all hours of the morning after a very long shift."

"No, we wouldn't. I'm worried about you putting in all these hours then going home and having to fend for yourself."

"I've done it all my life, I can't see it changing anytime soon, not unless you divorce that hunky husband of yours and send him in my direction."

"You're a trier, I'll give you that. Please consider what I've said."

"I have, and it's a thank you attached with a firm no. I can't and won't put you through living with my tough routine."

"The offer still stands, if you should change your mind. It's no bother at all."

"Thanks. Enjoy the rest of your evening, snuggled up to Mark. I have two corpses awaiting my attention."

"Can't you do one tonight and leave the other one until the morning?"

"Nope, I prefer to clear the decks, otherwise things have a habit of burying me. Goodnight, and thanks for checking in with me, Sara. You're a sweetheart."

"Take care. I'll speak to you tomorrow."

Sara hit the End Call button and threw her phone on the bed. She slipped out of her work clothes, had a quick wash, and then put on her leisure suit and went back downstairs to help Mark, not that he needed it. As usual, he had everything in hand.

"What can I do to help?"

"Lay the table and feed Misty, she's been wrapping herself around my legs for the past ten minutes. She's either hungry or trying her best to send me arse over tit."

Sara swooped down and cradled Misty in her arms like a baby. "You little minx, you're going to cause an accident one of these days."

Misty reached up and touched Sara's nose with her paw. Sara grabbed it and kissed it. She righted Misty once more and filled her bowl with a pouch of cat food and some chicken that was left over from the Sunday roast in the fridge.

"Hey, I had my eye on that for lunch tomorrow," Mark ribbed her.

"As if. Our pussy's needs are greater than yours."

He chuckled. "If you say so."

She slapped him playfully, saw to Misty's needs and laid the table as Mark had requested. Before long, they were tucking into their evening meal and discussing each other's day.

"Wow, I thought it was strange, you being concerned

about Lorraine. What a pickle to be in. Do you think you'll catch the bastard?"

Sara held up her crossed fingers. "We have to think positively about it. I'm annoyed that we had him in our grasp and let him go. Carla thinks I'm being foolish, blaming myself, but the facts are there for all to see. It's hard to dismiss, even for me."

"Hey, I'm coming down on Carla's side for a change, it's not often that happens. There's no way you could have known what he was like. He sounds a manipulative little squirt to me."

"Yeah, I think you're probably right. Enough talk about work now, do you have room for pudding?"

He patted his stomach and smirked. "Oh sorry, you're being serious, I thought you were talking in code for a second there."

"Smutty bugger. We have the washing up to do first."

"That won't take long, not if we do it together, then we can take a glass of wine and cheese and biscuits up to bed and have an early night."

"How could any girl resist an offer like that?"

CHAPTER 6

The team hadn't been at work long when the call came in. A body had been found, close to the hospital. Sara and Carla rushed to the scene. SOCO were there already. A marquee had been erected to shield the corpse from rubberneckers, and Lorraine was in attendance, too. Sara handed Carla a paper suit and booties. Both togged up, they entered the tent to find Lorraine crouched next to the victim.

"Shit! Is she a paramedic?" Sara asked after spotting the woman's recognisable uniform.

"She is. Her ID is on her badge. She should be easy to trace. I'm presuming she left the hospital and got attacked on the way home. Her body was found under the large bush outside by a friend of mine, a doctor on his way into work this morning." Lorraine passed Sara a card. "I've told him you'll be wanting a word with him."

Sara accepted the card and kept it in her hand, not wanting to wrestle with her suit to find a suitable pocket. "Jesus, why her? Why kill a bloody paramedic? Not that it matters what job she did. What the fuck is going on in this shitty world of ours? People like her spend their days caring for others, only to have her life cut short by a coward. Sickens me beyond words. I apologise for ranting."

Lorraine got to her feet. "I must admit, the same thought crossed my mind when I showed up."

"How was she killed?"

"Strangled. I'm presuming someone ambushed her as she passed, dragged her behind the shrubs and throttled her."

"Any signs of her fighting back? Skin under the nails to help us ID the killer?"

"No, there's nothing that I can see. We won't give up, though. I'll get the tech guys to carry out the necessary tests as usual."

Sara stared at the body of the young woman and shook her head. "I can't get over this. Why her? Anything else for us? Estimated time of death?"

"I'd put it to around eleven or thereabouts last night."

"It's in the middle of a housing estate, for goodness' sake. The killer took a risk, striking where he did. Correction, he or she. We'll get the house-to-house organised, see if one of the neighbours either heard or saw anything."

"I wouldn't have thought the latter," Carla said, "Wouldn't they have called it in?"

"Who knows?" Sara replied. "We'll let you know if we gather any information."

"We'll crack on, I want her out of here pronto. Hate the thought of people milling around outside, waiting for a glimpse of the body, knowing that she's one of us."

"I agree."

Sara and Carla left the tent and stripped off their protective suits.

"Get onto the station, ask the desk sergeant to flood the area with any available officers. I want this dealt with ASAP."

"Will do." Carla made the call on the way back to the car. "He's got it all in hand, was awaiting our call."

"Good old Jeff. Right, we need to have a word with the doctor who found her."

Sara drove the short distance to the hospital and parked on double yellow lines outside the main entrance. A security guard came out to tell her to move the car. She showed him her ID and told him they'd be twenty minutes at the most. He grudgingly accepted her reply, probably in light of what he'd heard about the victim. Generally, security guards on duty at the hospital weren't usually so obliging.

They stopped at the reception desk and asked to speak with the doctor who had found the body. He appeared after ten minutes and apologised for keeping them waiting. He showed them into a vacant room near the reception area.

Joel Reynolds was in his early thirties. He had worry lines creasing his forehead and a few greying hairs on both sides. "This is unbelievable. I found her, you're going to have my DNA all over her because I checked her body, searching for a pulse."

"Don't worry, I would be disappointed in you if you hadn't examined her. Did you know the victim?"

"Yes, Darcie Lockyear. She's a regular, coming in and out with patients to A and E all the time. Her work partner is sitting in a cubicle, he's devastated. I had to break the news to him this morning. He told me he'd tried to contact her as she was late for work, but his call went to voicemail. She was so cold, I'm presuming she was out there all night?"

"The pathologist believes she died at around eleven last night."

He nodded and sighed heavily. "I believe her shift ended at around ten-thirty. She always hung around, having a chat with the staff, rather than head home right away."

"Was there a reason for that? Was she married?"

"No, she got divorced about three months ago. We're all friends here, even the paramedics are regarded as part of the team, so it's natural that she should want to hang out after her shift."

"And her partner? What's his name?"

"Ian Alott. He left soon after his shift ended. He's got a wife and a young family at home, prefers to head off as soon as his shift has ended."

"Did you see anyone loitering, or showing an interest in what was going on, when you found her?"

"No. Hardly surprising, given the time of death, Inspector."

"I know. It's not uncommon for the killer to remain in the area after they've committed the crime, so it's always best to check."

"Ah, yes, I didn't realise that. No, there was no one around. I called nine-nine-nine as soon as I found her. Not what I was expecting to see first thing, I can tell you. Shoved under the bushes, she was. The killer did a good job of hiding her. If I hadn't spotted her hand poking out, who knows how long she would have lain there, undiscovered? I'm glad it was me who found her and not a bunch of kids on their way to school. What a shock that would have been for them. She was strangled, wasn't she?"

"Yes, as far as the pathologist can tell. We'll know more once the PM has been performed later today. Do you know if Darcie had any relatives living in the area?"

"I think you'd better ask Ian. I can take you to him, if you like? I'm going to need to get back to work soon. We've already got a backlog of patients to see, and there are only two doctors on duty today."

"Go, thanks for taking the time to talk with us. We're going to need to get a statement from you; maybe it will be better if you called into the station on your way home, how does that sound?"

"It won't be until gone eight this evening."

"Fine by us."

"Okay, as if my day isn't long enough, and this is me on the early shift for a change. Still, I'm prepared to do anything for Darcie, she was one of the special ones. I'll take you to see Ian now."

They followed the doctor through the corridor to the cubicles at the end. Ian was sitting in a chair, his hands covering his colourless face.

Sara and Carla produced their IDs, and Sara introduced herself.

"Hi, Ian. I'm Inspector Ramsey. I'm so sorry for the loss of your friend and colleague."

"When Joel told me, I didn't believe him. I tried ringing Darcie again, but when it went through to voicemail, well... you know the rest."

"We do. It's strange how we react when sad news is broken to us."

"I can't believe she's gone. I know she's had a rough year but she was getting her life back on the right path, only for this to happen. She didn't deserve this, no one does, not to go out like this, at the hands of a vile person with nothing better to do with their bloody days than to attack... or kill innocent women."

"We'll find the person responsible, I promise. Were you with her last night?"

"Yes, we finished our shift at around ten forty-five, fifteen minutes late, that's early for us. I said I couldn't hang around; she was okay with that. We left the hospital together, rather than have a coffee at the end of our shift with the other staff. I saw her to her car. She had trouble starting it and had to call a breakdown truck. I said I'd stay with her, but she was having none of it. That's the last I saw of her, and now… she's dead. I don't think I'm ever going to be able to forgive myself for leaving her last night. Why didn't I just stick around with her until the breakdown service arrived?"

"In my experience, blaming yourself isn't going to do you any good. Hindsight is a wonderful thing. It can also kick our backsides when we least expect it to. Any idea which breakdown service she rang?"

"It was a local one, sorry, I can't remember the name. She told me she'd used them before and they were always prompt and customer-oriented."

"Okay, there can't be too many in the area. Sergeant, can you get the team to try and trace the driver?"

Carla nodded and left the cubical.

Sara took a step closer to the distraught paramedic. "I know how difficult this must be for you right now, but has Darcie ever mentioned being in trouble? Or has someone pestered her and she's brushed off their advances, anything like that? The doctor told us that she'd recently got divorced. Does the ex-husband still live locally or has he moved away?"

"No, she never mentioned anything. We work twelve-hour shifts, there's no time for socialising, not really. Her ex-husband, Sean, he was a nice bloke, they're still really good friends. They struggled, or should I say, he struggled, to adapt to her shift patterns. Bugger, should I give him a ring, tell him she's… gone?"

Sara shook her head. "Don't worry, we can do that. Do you have his details?"

"He's still living at their old address, it's for sale. Darcie moved out because the opportunity of a flat she'd had her eye on for a while popped up, and he told her to jump at the chance of grabbing it."

"And the address is?"

"Hang on, it's in my contacts." He removed his phone

from his pocket and reeled off the address which Sara noted down in her pad.

"Great, and you definitely didn't sense there was any animosity between them?"

"Not at all. They've got a fifteen-year-old son, Chris. They made a pact that despite what had gone on between them that they would remain friends for the son's sake. They are, were, both genuinely nice people. Sean is going to be totally cut up by the news, poor bloke."

"We'll break it to him gently, don't worry. What about other family, did Darcie have anyone else living in Hereford?"

"Her mother, Amy. She's living in a hospice, I think. Please, I wouldn't advise telling her, the poor woman's dying of cancer."

"Oh no, that's dreadful. She'll have to be told. Maybe Sean will pass on the news for us."

"Yes, she adores him. Maybe that would be for the best."

"Going back to her car, did you notice if it was still in the car park or not?"

"It wasn't. So I presumed either she had got it started last night or they had towed it away. I should have checked in with her again last night before I dropped off to sleep. It was a long shift yesterday, and I was exhausted."

"Again, please don't keep going over things, what might have been, it's not going to do any good."

"I hear what you're saying, but my head is telling me otherwise."

Sara squeezed the man's shoulder. "I'm sorry. It's a tough situation to find yourself in."

"Tougher for Darcie, she's dead." His hands covered his face again, and he sobbed.

Saddened by the man's utter despair, Sara's heart sank.

Carla came back into the cubicle. "Does Dan's Breakdown's ring any bells with you?" she tentatively asked Ian.

He glanced up, his eyes reddened, and nodded. "Yes, that's the one. Why couldn't I think of that before?"

"Don't worry. You know as well as I do what shock can do to the mind and the body," Sara replied. "We're going to leave you now and get on with the investigation, unless there's anything else you can think of that we should know about?"

"There's not. Darcie put her heart and soul into this job, it wrecked her marriage, and now she's… gone. I'm mortified this should have happened to her."

"We'll get the person who did this, I promise we will."

"Good. I hope they rot in prison for the rest of their lives, or worse."

Sara and Carla left the cubicle and raced through the corridor back to the car.

"I'm not going to bother to ring to announce we're on our way, I'd rather show up and pay the service a surprise visit. We'll do that first and then whizz out to break the news to her ex."

Carla paused before getting into the car. "Her ex? How come?"

"She only has her mother and Ian told me that she's in a hospice. I couldn't do it to her."

"Shit! Was she still friendly with the ex?"

"Yes, and they have a fifteen-year-old son, too."

"God, this just gets worse, doesn't it? That poor family."

"Yeah, I don't want to dwell on it. Let's get going."

FIFTEEN MINUTES LATER, they drew up outside the breakdown garage. Two mechanics were working on a car, and there was a man in his thirties sitting in the office. Sara knocked on the door, and he looked up and motioned for them to join him.

"Can I help?"

Sara showed her warrant card. "DI Sara Ramsey and DS Carla Jameson. Are you Dan?"

He frowned. "I am. How can I help?"

"Would it be okay if we came in and had a word with you about an incident that took place last night?"

He pointed at the chair in front of him. "Sit down. There's another chair in the corner there," he told Carla.

Carla pulled it up to the desk.

"What type of incident are we talking about here?" he asked once they were both seated.

"A breakdown out at the hospital."

"Ah, yes. Darcie, she's used our services before. The guys are working on the car now. They only started half an hour ago. I think the prognosis is dicey to say the least. I don't understand what the problem is here and why the police are involved."

"Did you recover the vehicle last night?" Sara pushed ahead.

"One of my men did. Do you want to have a word with him?"

"If you don't mind."

He left his seat and opened the door to bellow, "Mick, got a sec, mate?"

A clean-shaven young man appeared in the doorway soon after. "Yes, Dan?"

"Come in and close the door. These two ladies are from the police. They'd like a word about Darcie's breakdown last night."

Mick wiped his hands on an oily cloth and inclined his head. "We're working on the car now. I told Darcie it might take a few days to fix it. What's the problem?"

"Do you usually try and fix cars at the roadside?" Sara asked. She noted the confusion on the young man's face.

"Yes, always, if we can. The car refused to start. In that instance, we tow it away and work on it the next day. Which is exactly what's happening out there. Why?"

"Can you run through the events as they occurred last night?"

"Darcie called us. I showed up, had a quick tinker with the car, but it refused to start. I told her I'd need to bring it in. Offered her a lift home, she turned me down, said she could do with the walk to clear her head after a stressful day at work, and that was it. I put the car on the flatbed and brought it back here."

"And Darcie set off on foot, is that right?"

"Yes. What's going on? Has something happened to her?" Mick asked, his eyes full of concern.

Sara inhaled a breath and let it out slowly. "Sadly, Darcie's body was found in the undergrowth, not far from the hospital this morning."

"Holy crap! Are you bloody serious?" Mick shouted.

"All right, calm down, mate," his boss said. "Is this true?" he asked Sara.

"Why would I make it up? Yes, it's true. We're trying to piece together what happened in her final hours. You left her in the car park, yes?"

Mick appeared shellshocked by the news. "Yes. I asked her twice if I could give her a lift home, and both times she refused. Jesus, this can't be right... her dying like this."

"Did you see anyone hanging around at all?"

"Not really, apart from a few cars coming and going to the hospital. I didn't see anyone walking, if that's what you're asking. Damn, that poor girl. I feel guilty now... I asked her if she wanted a lift; if she had said yes, she would have got home safely. I would have made sure of that."

119

"These things happen." Sara nodded. "We're going to need to take a statement from you in the next forty-eight hours."

"Of course, I'll do anything I can to help."

"We both will," his boss added, looking equally bamboozled by what Sara had revealed.

"What time did you show up there?"

"Around five to eleven. I left about eleven-ten," Mick confirmed.

"Thanks, it's good to get our timeline in order. Sorry to be the bearer of such sad news. Thanks for your help."

Mick shrugged. "I ain't done nothing but I could have done more last night."

Sara smiled.

His boss dismissed him and said, "Poor bloke is going to be cut up about Darcie, she was a lovely lady. Do you think she was specifically targeted, or was someone out on the prowl trying to get a cheap thrill and it went wrong?"

"We're not sure about that just yet. Our investigation is in its infancy. Lots of answers to seek before we can assess the case thoroughly. Thanks for your help."

"I hate to ask this, but what's going to happen with regards to her car? My lads can't be wasting time on it if they aren't going to get paid for the work at the end. Shit, that makes me sound a right bastard, putting my business before that lady's death."

Sara waved a hand. "It's a logical route to take. I would call it a day. I'm on the way to see the ex-husband now. I'll let him know the car is here and ask him to get in touch with you later, how's that?"

"Thanks, I appreciate it. Sorry we couldn't have been of further assistance. By the sounds of it, Mick did his best for the woman last night. Why do you women put up the barriers when some men go out of their way to offer help? The vast majority of you are too set in your ways these days.

Too independent for your own good. Not all men are bad, you know."

"I know. It's hard to fathom. We appreciate that Mick was trying to do the right thing by Darcie. Have a chat with him after we leave, make sure he's all right, will you? This wasn't his fault. If you can emphasise that for me, that would be great. We'll get out of your hair now. All right if I send a uniformed officer over to get a statement from Mick during the day? The quicker we get something down on paper the better."

"Yeah, okay, and don't worry, I'll make sure he's all right. This is going to knock him off his game, he's a good lad. Always treats the ladies well. He was brought up with three sisters, and his parents died when he was in his teens, so he's had to watch out for them over the years."

"That's a shame. He seems nice enough. Sorry to have dropped in on you like this and spoilt your day."

"I'm gutted we couldn't do more to help you out."

"If we come across anything else, we'll give you a ring. In the meantime, here's my card, if Mick thinks of something that might prove useful to the investigation."

He nodded, and Sara and Carla returned to the car.

"How awful, to be called out like that, offer to help, and then be told that the customer died not long after you were with them," Carla commented as they got back into the car.

"Life sucks, eh? Jesus, I'm getting sick and tired of having to share bad news with folks. That seems to be what fifty percent of our time consists of these days."

"You're not wrong. Still, chin up, duty calls. Are you up for another round of doom and gloom?"

Sara rolled her eyes and started the engine. "I'm going to have to be, there's no way around this one."

She drove to the address Ian had given her, but there was no one at home. Sara knocked next door at the neighbour's house, and an elderly woman told them that Sean worked in the city at a bank but she couldn't remember which one. Sara thanked the woman and jumped back in the car. She rang Jill at the station and requested that she call all the banks in the centre of town to see if Sean Lockyear worked there.

"We'll head over that way and grab a coffee in one of the cafés."

"I'll get back to you soon, boss. Have a latte on me while you're at it."

Sara smiled and ended the call. "Sounds like a mighty fine idea to me, and a sticky bun thrown in for good measure, too. What do you say, partner?"

"Is it on you?"

Sara tutted. "I suppose so."

WITH SARA and Carla now repleted, it wasn't long before Jill came up with the goods. "He works for NatWest in the centre, boss."

"We're up the road from there now, thanks, Jill. We'll be back shortly. Any news at that end?"

"I think the boys have a few leads regarding the car, but it's not for me to spoil their excitement."

"Sounds interesting. See you soon."

"It's about time something came our way," Carla said. "Umm… can I remind you that we're working not one or even two, but bloody three investigations now?"

Sara pulled a face. "I'm aware of that fact, thank you. And your point is?"

"I'm just saying that if there are too many balls in the air, something is bound to drop."

"Yeah, that's what I'm hoping, something will *drop* into our laps soon. See what I did there?"

Carla groaned, and they set off down the high street,

weaving in and out of the bustling crowd.

"It's market day."

"Is that why the stalls are here?" Sara grinned.

Carla groaned again. "I know when to keep quiet."

"Makes a change. You're learning." Sara opened the large door to the bank and headed towards a woman standing at one of the desks in the corner.

"Hi, how can I help you today?"

Sara flashed her warrant card. "I wanted a quick word with Sean Lockyear, is he around?"

"He's upstairs in one of the offices. May I ask what this is about?"

"It's a personal matter. If you wouldn't mind telling him we're here, thanks."

"I'll be right back. I'd rather make the call in private, so the customers don't overhear."

"Good idea."

She scampered off, used her keycard to enter the door that led to the staff-only area and returned with Sean a few minutes later. He appeared concerned by their visit.

"Hi, Jackie said you wanted to see me."

"That's right. Is there somewhere private where we can go?"

"I'll see if there's a room free."

Jackie tapped him on the shoulder. "Room two is free."

"Thanks, Jackie, you're a lifesaver."

The woman blushed and took a step back to let them pass.

Inside the room, Sean switched on the light and rearranged the chairs. "Take a seat. Can I get you a drink?"

Sara raised a hand. "No, we're fine, don't worry about us." She didn't speak again until the three of them were seated. "Thank you for agreeing to see us so promptly. I'm afraid I have some bad news for you."

His hand slapped against his cheek. "Oh no, it's not Chris, is it? Has he been knocked off his bike? I told him not to take it to school, he assured me he would be careful."

"No. Please, this has nothing to do with Chris. This morning we were called out to a crime scene close to the hospital."

"Shit! No, it's not Darcie, is it? Has she been hurt by a patient? I knew it would only be a matter of time. People are so angry down there these days. The staff are overwhelmed, they're doing their best, but for some folks, it's just not good enough, is it?"

Sara didn't have the heart to interrupt him. Instead, she waited for his rant to end and then jumped in. "It might well have been a patient, we don't really know."

"What was? Are you telling me that she was attacked?"

"Yes. Sadly, Darcie's body was found earlier this morning by a doctor."

"Her body? As in she's *dead?*"

"I'm afraid so. Her partner told us where to find you. He also said that Darcie's mother is in a hospice. She would usually be the one we shared the news with, what with her being Darcie's next of kin, but we were wondering if you could do that. Ian also said that there was no animosity between you and Darcie."

"There wasn't. We still loved each other, I simply couldn't hack her shift pattern any longer. Now you're here telling me that she's dead? How? Do you know who did it?" He left his chair and paced the floor, running his hand through his hair before returning to his seat. "Tell me, do you know?"

"We don't. Our main priority was to come here and break the news, then we'll begin the investigation in earnest."

"I can't believe what you're saying. How the hell does someone, a healthy woman, just die like that?"

"It would appear that someone strangled her. That was

the pathologist's initial assessment. We're awaiting the results of the post-mortem before we can say for definite. I have to ask, when was the last time you either saw or spoke to Darcie?"

"At the weekend, her last day off. She wanted to spend time with us, me and Chris. We went on a picnic as the weather was good. Chris even had a swim in the river, ever one for taking a risk as it was bloody freezing."

"Did she mention if anything was troubling her?"

"No, nothing. What are you saying? You think someone had it in for her? Someone stalked her?"

"We're not sure. It's an avenue we need to go down; it would be wrong of me not to ask such an obvious question."

He fell silent, his hand constantly running through his hair and intermittently travelling over his face. "I can't think of anyone, but then, who's to say what type of nutters she used to meet day in, day out, ferrying people to hospital? I know some of them were time-wasters who had nothing better to do than keep ringing up for an ambulance all the time, even if they developed a slight cough. It's despicable the way people treat the NHS these days. You go down to the A and E at any time of the day, and I doubt you'll see a single person bleeding out. That's how it used to be when I was a kid, that's the only time we were allowed near a hospital. Nowadays, I swear people go down there if they've got a minor headache or even an earache. They need to get a life and stop preventing the seriously ill folks from seeing a doctor for life-threatening treatment. Sorry, I know I shouldn't be going on like this… I suppose I'm in shock. To think, we were getting on so well together lately, I was going to ask her if she would be willing to move back home and give us another go." He sighed. "No fear of that happening now, is there?"

"That's a real shame. Sometimes people don't realise what

they have until it's too late." Sara bit down on her tongue and corrected herself. "I apologise, I was talking about you guys going through a divorce, only to see the light, not meaning now that she has passed away."

"I knew what you meant," he replied, to Sara's relief. "You're right. Couples tend to give up on their relationships far too easily these days, don't they? Move on to pastures new readily enough, without weighing up the pros and cons."

"It seems that way. Are you going to be okay?"

He shrugged and linked his hands together. "I don't know, it's going to be tough telling Chris."

"I can help you out, assign a family liaison officer to come and be with you for a few days, if you like?"

"No. We'll be fine. I think it would be worse having a stranger in the house. Chris is quite reserved, doesn't really like mixing with new people. What happens next?"

"We go back to the station and begin our investigation. Umm... going back to Darcie's mother, she should be told as her daughter's next of kin. I wondered if it would be inappropriate, or asking too much of you, if you might consider telling her mother for me."

"God, I never even thought about Iris knowing. Shit, she only has a few weeks to live herself, and now you want me to share the news that her only daughter has gone before her." Tears formed, and a stray one splashed onto his cheek. "I'm not sure I can. I mean, I know why you're asking me because you think the news would be coming better from someone she knows well, but even so... how can I break the woman's heart just before her own life ends?"

Sara swallowed down the bile that had emerged in her throat. "I'm sorry. I should never have asked. I just thought, in the dire circumstances, maybe the news would be better coming from someone close to her. Don't worry, I don't want to put you through any further stress. I can visit her after I leave here."

Sean stared at the floor for a few moments and then mumbled, "No, I'll do it. You're right, she wouldn't forgive me if I didn't tell her myself. That's both their hearts I'm going to break today, her son's and her mother's. What an utterly shitty day ahead of me."

"Would you rather we were there for moral support? We don't mind."

"No, I would prefer doing it myself while you're out there, searching for the evil bastard who has robbed this family."

"Is there anything you want to ask before we leave?"

"Yes, is she the only one to have been killed? I hear so many crazy things on the news these days, talk of a serial killer at large."

"At present, we believe that's not the case, however, once we start digging, who knows where the investigation will lead us?" Sara rose from her seat, and Carla followed.

Sean showed them to the front door.

"I hope you find them soon. I couldn't bear the thought of another family going through what I'm experiencing. It sucks, big time, to lose someone you loved in such a dreadful, pointless way."

"I can imagine. You have my word that we will do our very best to find this person swiftly. Take care of yourself. Here's my card. If you have any questions or if something else comes to mind, please don't hesitate to ring me, day or night."

He stared at the card for a moment or two and then glanced up at Sara again. "I'll have a think, see if anything crops up. I'm going to get the terrible deed out of the way now and visit the hospice."

"Good luck. Thank you for doing this for me, I appreciate

how tough a task it is going to be."

"I'll get one of the nurses to sit with me while I tell her, she's bound to take the news hard."

"That's a good call. Take care of yourself and your son. I'll be in touch soon, hopefully with some good news for you."

"Thanks." He offered up a slight smile and walked them back to the entrance.

On the way back to the car, Carla was unusually quiet.

"What's up?" Sara asked and then slipped into the driver's seat.

"Something he said got my brain working."

"Are you going to share with me what that was or are you asking me to guess?"

"Hmm… I'm probably overthinking things. But he asked if we had a serial killer on our hands."

"I heard him, I'm not deaf."

"All right, there's no need for you to snap at me. Think about it, all right, we can dismiss the second murder of Mrs Hanson because we've got an inkling of who killed her, but what about the other two investigations?"

Sara considered her partner's possibility for a few seconds. "Hmm… okay, you make a valid point. We've got a doctor mowed down outside his home and a paramedic who was strangled close to the hospital."

"I know, we don't generally believe in coincidences," Carla replied.

"You're right. Let's get back to base. I need to check if anything has come to light from the house-to-house enquiries. Let me think this over for a while, maybe run it past Lorraine as well."

"I'm glad you're considering taking it seriously. Of course, I might just have steered the investigations off route, but hey-ho, what else have we got to go on anyway, right?"

"Too true."

CHAPTER 7

*J*oel blew out an exhausted breath. He was at the end of his mammoth sixteen-hour shift. "That's a wrap for me, guys. I'll see you all in the morning at seven, and we'll do it all over again." He glanced at his watch. It was already one-ten in the morning. By the time he got home and made himself a drink to unwind, he'd probably catch four hours' sleep, if he was lucky. Something had to give. The hospital was now taking the piss. One long shift in a blue moon, the administrators had said. Now, putting in long shifts weekly had become the norm. They didn't care who manned the A&E department, as long as someone did.

"Off home now. Are you, Doc, or will you be stopping off at a nightclub on your way home?" one of the porters shouted as he left triage.

"These feet are going straight home to bed, they haven't got it in them to be boogying around the dance floor, Ned. See you tomorrow."

"I'll be here. Sleep well, Doc."

"Sleep? What's that?"

"Taking the mick they are with you, but you know my view on the subject."

"Yeah, not worth repeating ourselves, is it? Thanks for caring, mate." Joel stopped off at the locker room, collected his bag, and instead of getting changed, like he should have, he decided to wear his uniform home and slipped his padded jacket over the top. On his way out to the car, he caught up with the messages from friends who had tried to get in touch with him during the course of the day. "Jesus, two invites for this evening, and I didn't even get back to them. They're going to think I'm an ignorant git." He tapped out a message, copied it and sent it to both parties before he reached his car.

Once inside, he sought out a soothing disc to accompany him on the journey home and set off. He hadn't travelled far when his phone pinged, signifying that he'd received yet another message. The lights turned to red up ahead. He took the opportunity to check his phone and respond, if a response was needed. He smiled at the retort his best mate had given about his excuse for not joining the gang that evening. He then sent a witty reply of his own.

Just then the passenger door opened, and someone quickly climbed in beside him.

"What the fuck are you doing?"

The intruder lashed out with his fist, catching Joel on the jaw. His head thumped against the window. Dazed, he tried to speak, but the man hit him again, not once or twice, but three times until he was knocked unconscious.

* * *

HE KNEW he had to move swiftly. The lights would be changing soon. He ran around the car, dragged Joel's body out of the front, threw him into the back seat of the vehicle and slipped into the driver's seat around the time the lights changed to green. He expelled the breath he'd been holding in, relieved that everything had gone according to plan. Now all he had to do was get rid of his unconscious passenger.

He took a right at the lights and then a left at the next junction. The road led out of the city and into the country towards Ross-on-Wye. He wouldn't get that far, he knew exactly where he was heading. He drummed his fingers on the steering wheel, appreciating the doctor's taste in music. Peering into the back seat via the rear-view mirror, he smiled at his accomplishment. He had expected the doc to put up some kind of fight, but there was nothing. He was far too busy twiddling with that damn phone of his to be concerned about what was going on around him.

"Bloody idiot. People needed to be more alert, travelling alone, in the dead of the night." He laughed at his own joke and relaxed his head back against the padded headrest. "Nice car. Shame really. I wouldn't have minded keeping this one for myself. Them's the breaks."

The clearing he had spotted earlier, and checked out for a possible dumping site, came into view up ahead. He indicated, not that there were any other cars around at this time of the morning. His own car was already here. He parked around ten feet away from it and got out of the vehicle. He opened the back door to check his hostage was still out cold. He was. Then he crossed the muddy car park to his own vehicle and removed the petrol can from the boot.

Once he'd covered the doctor's car in the liquid, he tapped on the window in the back to gain the doctor's attention. It took a while, but eventually the doctor came around and sat upright and stared at him. He waved and then removed a couple of matches from the box, struck them, and then threw them onto the roof of the car and ran. He would have loved nothing more than to hang around to see the doctor fry, but his need to get away far outweighed his inquisitiveness.

CHAPTER 8

*S*ara was up and eating a slice of toast when the call came in. "DI Sara Ramsey."

"Sorry to trouble you so early, ma'am, it's Jeff."

"No problem, Jeff. What's wrong?"

"We've got a suspicious death on the outskirts of the city, and I wondered if you wanted to take it on."

"Jesus, man, isn't three different investigations enough for me and my team to be dealing with at present? Isn't there anyone else available?"

"It's the cutbacks, ma'am. I can ask, but looking at the rotas, we've got a few bodies off on holiday and…"

"All right, I'll do it. You owe me, though."

"Of course, ma'am."

"Give me the details."

"Out on the A49, on the Ross road at Much Birch, or just outside." He furnished her with the postcode to enter into her satnav. "Do you need me to give Carla a call?"

"Yes, get her to meet me out at the location. I'll just finish up here and be on the road in five minutes."

"I'll get onto her now. Again, thanks for taking the case on. I had a feeling you wouldn't turn me down."

"You're lucky I'm in a good mood today, otherwise it could have worked out differently for you."

He laughed, and Sara ended the call. She finished her coffee and turned to rinse her cup in the sink. Mark slipped his arms around her waist and rested his chin on her shoulder.

"Did I hear you on the phone?"

She swivelled to face him, and they shared a kiss. Misty meowed at their feet, shouting for her breakfast.

"You did. I've been called out to another suspicious death."

Mark frowned and took a step back. "What? That's taking the piss, Sara. You're snowed under as it is. Can't they get someone else to attend the scene and take on the case?"

"Don't worry, I asked the same question. Jeff sounded embarrassed when he told me that there isn't anyone else available because of staff holidays."

"Jesus, don't you guys confer? Isn't there any structure in that station? Why take off at the same time?"

She touched a hand to his face. "I don't know the ins and outs of it, love. Don't worry, I'll be having a word with the chief later, time permitting. I'm going to have to love you and leave you. Damn, I haven't fed Misty yet."

He tutted and kissed her on the lips. "Don't worry, I'll do it. Give me a call during the day if you get five minutes. On second thoughts, don't, I doubt if you'll get five minutes, and if you do, you'll want to top up your caffeine levels."

"That goes without saying. There's nothing stopping me giving you a call at the same time. I'm a woman, I can multi-task, don't you know?"

They both laughed, and Sara kissed Mark on the cheek and headed for the door.

"Take care out there," he called after her.

"I'll be fine, don't worry about me. Have a good day. I hope that St Bernard doesn't get the hump with you when you castrate him."

"I'll watch out for that, don't worry. I mean it, no messing about, take care. Keep alert at all times."

Sara saluted him. "Yes, boss. I will, don't worry. And there's no need for you to be distracted either. Your job is equally as important as mine, and I can do without your mind wandering elsewhere."

"Don't worry. I have no intention of castrating the wrong dog. My nurse will keep me in line."

"Glad to hear it. Why don't we grab a takeaway tonight? I'll give you a call when I'm leaving the station."

"Why not? We haven't indulged for a few weeks. What do you fancy?"

Sara bit back her usual retort and slipped on her coat. "Indian, I think, but I'll leave it up to you."

"Sounds good to me. Love you. All right, Misty, let's get you fed."

"Love you more," she called back and left the house.

As it was reasonably early, the drive through Hereford and out through the other side of the city was pretty much stress-free as the traffic hadn't had a chance to build up yet. Because Carla lived closer to the city, she was already at the location, along with a couple of uniformed officers who had cordoned off the area, surrounding the burnt-out vehicle.

"Ouch. What the heck do we have here?" Sara got out of the car and asked, her gaze drawn to the vehicle, or what was left of it.

"A body was found on the back seat, burnt to a cinder. There's enough of the plate left, so I've got onto the station. I'm waiting on a call back."

"Don't tell me, there's going to be a delay because of the cutbacks?"

Carla sighed and rolled her eyes. "You guessed it."

"If I hear that sodding word once more this week, this month, this year, I'm going to tear my hair out."

"All right, calm down. I can tell you're in one of your moods, there's no need to take it out on me."

Sara gawped at Carla then closed her mouth. "For your information, partner, I am not, I repeat I am not, in one of my moods. I might be a tad pissed off that we got the call when no one else is available but I'll be having a word with Price about that later. Something needs to be sorted. As a team, we're stretched to the limits as it is, without taking on yet another case."

"I hear you, but what are you going to do? Refuse to investigate what is clearly a murder case? You won't, I won't let you."

"Get you. Of course I won't. I've shown up at the scene, haven't I?"

"Granted, but in a foul mood."

Sara stamped her foot. "I am not. But if you keep telling me I am, then yes, that will be the outcome. I take it the Forensics Team are on their way?"

"Yes, they've been notified. Not sure if they're on their way or not."

"I'll give Lorraine a call, gee her up. Who found the car?"

Carla pointed at a couple with two dogs lying at their feet. "Dog walkers. I've had a quick word. There was no one else in the area."

"Okay, get their details and let them go. My take is the fire happened last night, not first thing this morning."

"I was working along those lines, too. I'll have a chat."

Carla drifted over to the couple.

Sara kept an eye on what was going on as she placed the

call to Lorraine. "Hey, it's me. Are you on your way?"

"Yes, give me a chance. I had to stock up the van first. I should be with you within half an hour."

"Good. It's a nasty one."

"How many victims?"

"One from what I can tell. Who knows what we'll find in the boot?"

"Bugger, don't say that. Why throw that one into the mix?"

"I don't know. Pissed off maybe because the body count is rising this week."

"Pissed off in general by the sound of it. Let me crack on, and I'll be with you shortly. My team is ready to rumble. They'll be with you soon, and I won't be far behind them."

"Good. It's cold, damp and miserable out here. I'll wait in the car until you get here."

"What do you want, sympathy?"

"If I did, I doubt if any would be coming from your direction, would it?"

"You've got it, lady."

"Okay, see you soon."

She ended the call and then trotted back to the car, only making it by seconds before a huge downpour covered the area. Carla joined her moments later, cursing a thousand expletives under her breath.

Straight-faced, Sara said, "What the hell! It's only a drop of rain, it won't kill you."

"Well, I don't see you standing around out there in it. Furthermore, we can do without it washing away the evidence."

"Touché, you're right. Were they okay?"

"Yeah, happy not to be standing around in the weather. She was more upset than him. I thanked them and sent them on their way."

"I feel for her. Such a grisly find to stumble upon when you're out for a walk."

"How long are we going to have to hang around here?" Carla sat forward and peered up at the black clouds lingering overhead.

Sara raised an eyebrow and faced her partner. "As long as it takes. Lorraine is setting off now, and the rest of the team should be here in a matter of minutes." She turned the engine over and put the heater on, and the radio came to life, combatting the silence. She rested her head back, and that was the last she remembered.

CARLA NUDGED her elbow a few minutes later. "Hey, I thought you had dozed off."

"Me? Never. I was resting my eyes while I pondered the situation."

"Not sure who you're trying to convince, but it hasn't worked on me, just saying. Anyway, they're here, or should I say the team are."

"Has the station got back to you yet with an ID for the owner?"

"Not yet. I was going to give it another few minutes before I start jumping up and down."

"There's no need for that. A little compassion for people doing their best in extreme circumstances wouldn't go amiss, Sergeant."

Carla's chest inflated and deflated a few times, but she didn't respond verbally.

"Okay, make the call," Sara ordered. "I'll have a word with the team, see how long Lorraine is going to be." She hopped out of the car and approached the team's van. "Hi, guys. Any idea how long Lorraine is going to be now?"

"She should only be a few minutes, she got held up in the

traffic behind us. Some smart alec tried to jump the lights in town and got smacked in the side by a lorry."

"Dickhead. We're trying to track down the owner, going by what's left of the plate number. We haven't touched anything. I wanted to get the person's ID ASAP so we can inform the family before it appears on the news."

"Want me to have a shufty inside?" Brian asked. The tech had been working alongside Lorraine for a few years now.

"Would you mind?"

He finished pulling on a suit and booties and then ducked under the tape and peered into the car. Sara followed him but remained outside the tape, not seeing any point in getting suited up only to strip it off again to sit in the car until Lorraine arrived, which could be a while. She craned her neck to see what Brian was up to. He stepped away from the car empty-handed and walked back to share the news.

"Sorry, it's hard to find anything in there. I could only make out that it was a male, if that helps." He grinned.

"A great help, thanks for that. I'll be in the car. Give me a shout once you're set up."

"Will do. Lorraine should be here by then."

Carla was still on the phone as Sara trudged back to the car. She made it inside before another deluge came down. "Damn weather. Give us a bloody break. It has rained on and off for a solid two weeks now, and I'm sick to death of it."

"That's fantastic news, I'll pass it on to the boss. Cheers." Carla jabbed the End Call icon and dropped her phone onto her lap. "I've got it, eventually."

"And?"

"It's a Joel Reynolds. His address is thirty-four Mortlake Crescent, Warham in Hereford."

"That's a start, I suppose." Something caught her eye out of Carla's window. "Ah, here she is now." She left the vehicle with Carla close behind her. Thankfully, the rain had dulled to a fine mist. "I didn't think you were ever going to get here," she ribbed her pathologist friend.

Lorraine jumped out of the van and marched to the rear. She wrenched open the doors and glared at Sara. "Don't start."

"Sorry, I'm guilty of trying to make light of a dire situation."

"Well, don't. Someone lost their life here today. That's never something to be taken lightly."

Sara slapped her wrist. "I know. Forgive me. Brian took a gander at the body for me to see if he could find any ID. He couldn't. But, we're in luck, we ran the partial plate through the system. It took a while for them back at base to obtain the result, but we've just heard that the owner of the vehicle is a Joel Reynolds."

Lorraine froze. She stopped flinging her equipment around the back of the van, took a step back and stared at Sara, and then her gaze drifted over to the victim's vehicle. She uttered one word. "Shit!"

Sara grabbed Lorraine's forearm. "What are you saying? That you know him?"

"Yes. Fuck, he's a doctor at the hospital." She turned and sank onto the step of the van.

"Are you all right, Lorraine?"

"No, yes, I don't know. He's a good friend. A decent man. One of the best doctors I know, and now, he's gone."

"Jesus, I'm so sorry for your loss."

Lorraine suddenly bounced onto her feet and ran towards the group of bushes ahead of her where she emptied her stomach. Sara wasn't sure how to react, she'd never seen her friend in this kind of state before, not about a victim.

Carla joined Sara and whispered, "What's going on?"

"She knows him. He's a doctor at the hospital. Oh fuck, it's all slotting into place now. Joel, we spoke to a doctor in the A and E department only yesterday, you remember, when we paid Darcie's partner a visit? I'm sure that was his name."

"I could do a search on the hospital website."

"Yes, do it."

Carla got to work. Sara walked towards Lorraine but stopped after taking a few steps, not sure if she was doing the right thing or not, intruding on her friend's grief.

Lorraine must have sensed her coming because she snuck a look over her shoulder and shouted, "I'm fine. Just leave me alone for a few minutes."

Sara retraced her steps to see what Carla had come up with.

She angled the phone in Sara's direction. "He's the only Joel on the staff."

Sara closed her eyes and nodded. "That's him." There was something lingering at the back of her mind that was refusing to come forward. She thought long and hard, all the while keeping a watchful eye on Lorraine a few feet away from them. "Shit!" she whispered. "I remember now. The Hanson case. I think I'm right when I say this, but Lorraine told me that her friend in A and E had rung her specifically with a request to carry out the PM on Paul Hanson's mother."

"What? This is incredible. What does it all mean?"

Sara shook her head, her mind racing through the facts darting around it. "Going back to what you asked, whether the cases could be connected, I'm wondering if you might be right."

"Which ones?"

Sara stared at Carla and shrugged. "How about all of them?"

"No way, all four victims, that's a bit of a stretch, Sara."

"Is it? The first vic was a doctor. Then the second was a paramedic… same field of expertise, if you like. We'll dismiss

Mrs Hanson for the time being. Now we've got a fourth victim who is also a doctor."

"Shit! I know, I'll call the medical centre, see if Hanson was Dr Blake's patient."

"Or his mother, check that info as well, while you're at it."

Carla wandered back to the car to make the call. Sara took a few tentative paces towards Lorraine to see if she was okay.

"Stay back, it's not pretty over here," her friend warned.

"I've seen worse. I'm worried about you. Here, I've got a tissue if you need one." Sara pulled a packet from her pocket and offered it to Lorraine.

"Christ. Don't you ever take no for a frigging answer?" Lorraine snatched the packet and was all fingers, trying to get a tissue out.

She passed it back to Sara who obliged and handed her one. Lorraine blew her nose and wiped it, then threw the tissue behind the bush.

"I'll pretend I didn't see that, you litter lout."

"It's a tissue, it'll break down naturally, especially in this rain. Why him? He was such a decent chap. Loved his work, gave up a lot of his social life to be on shift at that damn hospital, to end up like this. I can't believe someone would do that to him."

"I thought it was intentional," Sara said and bit down on her lip for stating the obvious.

Lorraine either decided to brush over the faux pas or chose to ignore it.

Carla joined them, slightly out of breath. "You're never going to believe this."

"Hanson and his mother were patients of Blake, right?" Sara said, her heart hammering.

Carla frantically nodded.

"Would someone care to enlighten me as to what you're

going on about?" Lorraine asked. She headed back to her van and removed a protective suit from its plastic sleeve.

"Hey, you can't do this." Sara placed a hand over her friend's. "Get someone else to work the scene, you're not up to it, Lorraine."

"Who said I'm not? I wouldn't want to pass this case over to anyone else anyway. I'd only be letting Joel down if I did that. Stop avoiding the subject and tell me what you two are going on about."

"Something clicked after we found out who the latest victim was, and Carla has just carried out some extra digging for me."

Lorraine gestured with her hand for Sara to get on with it.

"All right, Miss Impatient. I'm getting there, if you'll give me a chance."

"I won't warn you again," Lorraine snapped.

"It was something you said about the Hanson case the other day."

"What about it? What did I say?"

"You told me that your friend," Sara glanced over her shoulder at the burnt-out vehicle behind them, "Joel, had asked you to perform a PM on Paul Hanson's mother, right?"

Lorraine frowned and seemed utterly confused. "Am I supposed to know where this is leading?"

"Okay, it got me thinking about all the investigations we have right now. What if they're all connected?"

"How?"

"Carla rang the medical centre where Dr Blake, the first victim, worked, and asked if the Hansons were his patients, and yes, they were."

"Fuck. Have you found this dickhead yet, or is he still on the run?"

"The latter, but it's only a matter of time before we catch

up with him, Lorraine," Sara assured her, somewhat lacking in confidence.

"You'd better. So, what you're saying is he's the one carrying out these killings? Why?"

"No idea. He appears to be targeting those who worked for the NHS, two doctors and a paramedic so far."

"Un-frigging-believable. I knew there was something off about that guy the second I laid eyes on him."

Sara gulped. "Umm… if that's the case, then we need to take the threats he made towards you very seriously indeed."

"Why? I don't work for the NHS, I'm with the Home Office."

"I know that, and so do you, but will he?" Sara countered. "What if he's bumping off those who were connected with his mother's death?" Another thought occurred to her. She withdrew her notebook from her pocket and handed it to Carla. "Look up the phone number of Ian, the paramedic. Give him a call, see if he and Darcie were the ones who transferred Hanson's mother to hospital when she died."

Carla flicked through the book and jabbed her finger at the page. "Here it is. I'll ring him and see." Her partner stepped away from them.

Sara turned back to find Lorraine with her head in her hands.

"Hey, what's wrong?" Sara asked, squeezing her shoulder.

"If only I had voiced my concerns to you sooner, we wouldn't be in this shit today, would we?"

"This isn't about apportioning the blame, love. We need to consider how we're going to catch this bastard, and quickly. There's no telling who he might kill next… the nurses at the hospital? Thinking about it, maybe not, his mother died at home, not when she got to the hospital."

"It's a possibility. What about the surgery? The receptionists or nurses down there? You're going to have to make everyone aware, Sara. Do it now. He's out there, for all we know, hiding, watching, or even stalking his next target."

"You're right. Okay, I'm going to call an emergency press conference, get his face circulated. If he's still in the area, as we suspect, then we need to do all we can to flush the evil shit out into the open."

"Great idea. Now, if you'll excuse me, I need to get on and deal with my friend."

"I still think you're wrong, taking this case on, hon. But you're not likely to listen to me, are you?"

"It's not a case of ignoring your advice… oh, I don't know. My mind is so confused right now."

"As expected. Here's Carla now. Shit, I recognise that look, she's about to deliver something that's going to blow our heads apart."

"That obvious, is it?" Carla caught the tail end of their conversation. "Yes, it took a while to check his schedule. He didn't recognise the Hanson name to begin with, then it all came flooding back to him. They were the ones who transported Mrs Hanson to the hospital."

"Fuck! Sometimes I hate being right, and this is one of those frigging moments. Right, we're going to have to love you and leave you, Lorraine. I need to organise a press conference ASAP, and in person. Are you sure you're going to be all right here? Dealing with Joel?"

"Yes, go. Don't worry about me. I'll click into professional gear once I get started. I have a great team around me whom I can rely on if things take a turn for the worse."

"All right, I hate to leave you and run, but needs must in a case like this. I'll check in with you later, let you know of any developments. If you'll do the same?"

"Of course. Now go, get out of my hair, it's damn well driving me to distraction today as it is."

"That's the spirit. Chin up. I'll be in touch soon."

On the way back to the car, Carla was quiet.

Sara stared at her. "Okay, what's on your mind?"

"I'm perturbed that you haven't done something and if I speak out of turn, I'm worried what the recriminations might be."

Sara stopped and slapped Carla's arm. "Come on, out with it! Do you really think that little of me that you're afraid to tell me what's laying heavily on your mind?"

"It's not, not really."

"You might want to tell your face that."

"Bugger, the trouble with you is, you can fecking read me like a goddamn book."

"I can. Now spit it out and make it snappy, I'm on a mission."

"I believe it's because you have your mind set on putting together the press conference that you've overlooked the obvious."

"Riddles and going round in circles spring to mind. Spill, Carla, pronto, mate."

"What about Lorraine?"

Sara glanced back at Lorraine who was hesitantly approaching the victim and then back at Carla. Puzzled, she asked, "What about her? I told her she should get someone else in to handle the scene. You heard her, she's having none of it."

"I heard. No, I meant... what about Lorraine and her safety?"

Sara's frown deepened. "Will you get to the point?"

"If I have to spell it out to you, I will. Two doctors, a paramedic, who all had a connection to Paul Hanson, not forgetting his own mother thrown into the mix. He is our prime suspect, isn't he?"

"He is, or he was, the last time I looked."

"You still don't get it, do you?"

"Get what?" Sara sighed, her impatience at breaking point.

"Lorraine carried out the PM on his mother and has also been threatened by the guy. Jesus, Sara, we should be protecting her at least until we've got this arsehole locked up, shouldn't we?"

Sara thumped her thigh, hard. "Fuck, you're right. I did mention to her that she needed to be more vigilant but... I get the impression she's going to brush off that advice. We're going to need to go ahead and get something organised all the same. She's not going to like it."

"Tough. I think it's a necessity, don't you?"

"Yes. You're right, it's a matter of urgency now."

"I know, you have your mind on capturing the bastard, but we still need to take care of the obvious."

"You're right. I'll run it past her now."

"If you want to risk her tearing you off a strip in public." Carla peered over her shoulder at Lorraine.

"Fair point." Sara continued her walk towards the car. "She ain't going to like it either way, is she?"

"Nope, but then, I doubt if she's ever had a serial killer on her tail before either."

"Granted. Come on, let's get on the road." Sara slipped behind the steering wheel and took a moment to study Lorraine and her reactions. "I don't care what she says, I can tell when she's not coping well. And that's a woman on the brink. The shit is going to hit the fan when she hears about our plan."

"Like you say, shit happens. If we manage to keep her safe, I'm sure she'll forgive us."

"That remains to be seen. I'll need to run this past the chief when we get back."

· · ·

147

BACK AT THE STATION, they tore up the stairs.

"You go on ahead and bring the team up to date, I shouldn't be too long." Sara didn't wait for a response, she took off towards DCI Price's office.

Mary glanced up as she entered the room. "Hello, Inspector Ramsey. Was she expecting you?"

"No, I was hoping she might be able to slot me in. It is a borderline emergency, if that will get me in there quicker."

Mary smiled and left her chair. She winked and said, "Let me see what I can do for you."

Sara smiled and paced the area until Mary returned. She was longer than Sara anticipated which made her doubt her reason for coming there.

Eventually, Mary appeared and gestured for Sara to join her. "Sorry, she was on the phone."

"No need to apologise. Thanks, Mary."

"Coffee?"

"That would be wonderful, I was beginning to think my throat had been cut. It's already been a long morning."

"Sorry to hear that. I'll bring it in."

"Hello, Sara," DCI Price said with a wary expression. "I'm somewhat surprised to see you. It must be serious if you've turned up unannounced."

"You know I wouldn't pester you if I didn't need to, boss."

"Come in. Sit down and tell me what's on your mind."

Sara made herself comfortable in the chair, but even then, as she relayed what was running through her mind, she fidgeted nonstop. She took a sip from the coffee Mary had delivered not long after she had taken her seat, then she summed up the situation as concisely as possible and ended it by saying, "I know Lorraine isn't going to like it, but I feel it's a necessity to protect her, given what we believe has happened to the other victims."

"And you definitely believe this Paul Hanson is your man?"

"So it would seem. We won't know that for sure until either we stumble across evidence linking him to each of the scenes or we catch up with him and he makes a full confession during an interview. At the moment, the likelihood of that occurring is bloody zilch."

"Have you considered holding a press conference?"

"I have, that's why we've come back to base. I know I should have dropped by and broken the news to Joel's next of kin but first, we need to find out who that is. Carla's dealing with that as we speak. But I also felt the need to bring you up to date and grab a piece of advice before I go any further."

"You're juggling a lot of balls in the air, Sara, I'm glad you dropped by to include me. I would have been disappointed in you if you hadn't. While I appreciate how professional you are, there are times, such as this, when things are likely to take a tumble if certain elements aren't secured into place."

"That was my thinking behind coming to see you. I wanted to make sure you were on board with the plan to offer Lorraine protection before I went ahead and sanctioned it."

"There was no need for you to do that, Lorraine is regarded as one of our own, we go the extra mile for those in the police family, don't we?"

Sara smiled. "That's what I thought. Although, us arranging it and her agreeing to be shadowed are two entirely different things."

They both laughed, and for the first time that morning, Sara felt the stress ease, if only for a second or two.

"I'm sure she'll see sense eventually. If you need any help making any arrangements, let me know, won't you? As you can see, I'm snowed under, make that drowning, in paperwork at present, but I'm also champing at the bit to get involved."

"My morning paperwork is still sitting in a neat pile in my bulging in-tray. Oops, maybe I shouldn't have admitted that."

"Too late. I'm willing to forgive you, especially with the number of open cases you're dealing with right now. Do you have enough staff to cope with the pressure?"

Sara raised an eyebrow. "And if I said no, would you miraculously conjure up another couple of bodies for me?"

Carol Price squirmed in her seat. "Er… yeah, maybe forget I asked that daft question."

"The cutbacks are a nightmare for all departments, and I can't see it getting better anytime soon. The government need shooting, making us work under these conditions when the crime rates are on the rise."

"Hey, you're preaching to the wrong person, I'm totally on your side. Now, what's your next step?"

"To sort out the press conference, and while that's being arranged, Carla and I will grow a pair of wings each and fly out to break the news to Joel's next of kin."

"Okay, you have more than enough on your plate. Let me get things organised with regard to protection for Lorraine. That way, I can be the one she chooses to shoot down in flames when she finds out what has been arranged behind her back. How is she coping?"

"She looked broken when we left her at the crime scene. I tried to tell her she was doing the wrong thing, being there, if she knew the victim, but she was having none of it. I suppose I can see her point, wanting to treat her friend respectfully when another pathologist might not. But all the same, it's a tough situation to deal with, one that I wouldn't envy, that's for definite."

"Nor me. Poor cow. They're understaffed over there as well, aren't they?"

"Correct. Who isn't these days?"

"Leave it with me. I've wasted enough of your valuable time as it is. Give me a call if something else comes to mind and you need any further assistance." Carol smiled. "This sounds bad, but I'm actually enjoying myself, for a change."

Sara rolled her eyes and stood. "The trouble is, you've been tucked up behind that desk for too long. If I didn't get out there every day and only had paperwork to deal with day in and day out, I think I would lose my mind within a month."

Carol jerked and pulled a funny face. "I'm not sure what you're insinuating, Inspector. I'm perfectly fine." She ended her pretend spasm with her tongue hanging out the corner of her mouth.

"If you insist, boss." Sara laughed and left the room. "You might want to check on the chief in a few minutes, she was acting weirdly. I thought it best to leave her to it."

Mary frowned and then laughed. "Is she winding you up again?"

"Honestly, it's hard to tell sometimes."

Sara waved and opened the door. "Have you got the men in white coats on speed dial? If not, it should be on your to-do list, Mary."

"I'll action it right away, Inspector. Thanks for the heads-up."

Sara chuckled her way back to the incident room where she found the team hard at it. "Any luck, Carla?"

"Finalising the details now. He was living with a Rita Caffey. A member of staff at the hospital told me she runs a beauty salon in the city. I'm in the process of ringing around them now, yet to find the right one."

"Okay, I'll crack on and organise the press conference for later as discussed. I'll be in my office, should you need me."

Carla nodded and spoke to a person on the phone.

Sara drifted into her office and took a second or two to take in the view of the Brecon Beacons. It had been a while since she had been up there, too long, in fact. She'd need to remedy that soon. She felt sure Mark would be up for the trip, possibly go away for the weekend in the near future.

Damn, not this weekend, though, a family meeting is looming.

She took her seat and rang Jane Donaldson, the press officer. "Jane, hi, it's Sara Ramsey, can you talk?"

"You've caught me between jobs. What can I do for you?"

"How are you fixed for pulling an emergency press conference, or am I pushing the boundaries of our friendship?"

Jane laughed. "I can probably get one organised within a few hours, if you're desperate."

"I am, extremely. I've got a serial killer on the loose, and it would seem he's gone to ground. We could do with flushing him out before he adds to the victim list."

"Damn. Leave it with me ten minutes, I'll see if I can pull in a few favours."

"I knew I could count on you, Jane."

"I'll get back to you."

"I have to pop out to break some bad news to a next of kin. You can either call me or text me on my mobile, if that's all right?"

"You've got it. I'll be in touch soon. Good luck."

"Thanks." Sara hung up and left her office to rejoin the rest of the team. "What about CCTV footage, guys? Anyone dealing with that?"

"I put Craig and Barry on it," Carla shouted.

"We're running through the footage now, boss. Nothing showing up so far," Barry responded.

"Stick with it. As soon as you have anything, let me know."

Barry raised his thumb and concentrated on the screen once more.

Sara lingered by Carla's desk. She heard her partner tut a couple of times, unsure if the gesture was aimed at her or not. She moved over to the whiteboard and brought that up to date with the latest victim's details. Carla joined her a few minutes later.

"I've got her."

Sara finished off the points she was noting down, and then they left the incident room.

"Did you speak to her?"

"No, I asked a member of staff if she was the owner. They confirmed that she was on the premises, and I ended the call."

"Good."

Once they reached the car, Carla asked, "How did you get on with the press officer?"

"She should be calling me back in a few minutes. She's hopeful one can be arranged for this afternoon."

"Good. And the issue regarding Lorraine?"

"It's out of my hands."

"Meaning?"

"DCI Price is dealing with it. She's eager to lend a hand on this one. I've agreed as we're definitely under the cosh."

"Blimey, you actually admitted you were struggling to her?"

"I wouldn't put it quite like that myself, but yes, words to that effect. She agreed with me that Lorraine should be protected at all times."

Carla sucked in a breath. "She ain't gonna like it."

"I don't think she's got a choice, not now the chief agrees with me."

"We'll see. Take a right here, and we should be able to park in Waitrose car park and walk to the salon, which I believe is just around the corner."

Sara indicated and parked at the far end of the car park, close to the shopping mall as opposed to the supermarket entrance, where it was far busier.

She left a note on the windscreen explaining that they were on official business, and they set off on foot.

The salon was relatively busy when they arrived. A pretty blonde came to assist them as soon as they stepped through the front door.

"Hi, do you have an appointment?"

Sara flashed her warrant card and matched the woman's smile with one of her own. "We don't. Is Rita Caffey around?"

"Oh, I see. Yes, she's in the office."

Sara's smile broadened. "Would you mind asking her if she has time to see us?"

"Of course. Wait there. I'll be right back." She scampered off, mumbled something as she passed the other two girls tending to customers in the main salon, and then she disappeared out the back.

The other two beauticians both looked their way. Sara turned her back on them. The receptionist came back a few minutes later with a woman in a sleek black suit and high heels that could do some damage to a person if aimed in the right place.

"I'm Rita. How can I help you, ladies?"

"It would be better if we held our conversation in private, Miss Caffey."

She turned on her spiky heels and in a tone that matched her shoes, she called over her shoulder, "Very well. Come this way."

They followed her through the salon under the scrutiny

of the staff and customers into an office decked out in black-and-chrome furniture that glinted under the elaborate chandelier.

"Take a seat. Now what is this concerning? Make it quick, I have a very important Zoom meeting I need to make with a supplier in ten minutes."

"We shouldn't hold you up too long."

She sat in her executive leather chair and linked her hands in front of her. "Okay. Has the salon done anything wrong to warrant the police showing up on my doorstep?"

"No, our visit has nothing to do with the salon, Miss Caffey."

"You can call me Rita. Then I don't understand why you're here."

Sara inhaled a steadying breath and said, "It is with regret that we have to share some grave news with you."

Rita's eyes narrowed. Sara wondered if she'd had Botox, which would explain why her brow hadn't wrinkled.

"Concerning?"

"Your boyfriend, Joel."

"Oh, him. What about him?"

"Umm… by the sounds of it, you seem a little miffed by him, would that be correct?"

"Miffed? That's one word for it, I suppose. No, if you must know, I'm pretty pissed off with him."

"May I ask why?"

"Because it was my birthday yesterday, and he switched shifts rather than take me out to dinner, then he had the audacity to work right through the night without even ringing me to let me know he was doing an extra shift. Too right I'm pissed off with him, how dare he treat me like that?"

Carla nudged Sara's knee slightly.

Sara prepared herself for the onslaught of tears and grief she assumed the woman was about to unleash once Sara delivered the news. "As I said, we've come here today to share some grave news."

"Oh yes, you did say that. And what might that be? No, Joel hasn't been attacked while he was on duty, has he? Shit, I'll never forgive myself for thinking badly of him if he has, and why hasn't anyone from the hospital rung me before this? Come on, out with it. What's happened to him?" Her tone went up a notch with every question she asked.

"It is with regret that I have to tell you that Joel lost his life in the early hours of this morning."

Rita froze for a second or two and then let out an ear-bursting scream that made Sara jump. Rita continued to fill her lungs, over and over until her voice gave in. Her head collapsed onto her arms on the desk, and she sobbed.

Sara and Carla stared wide-eyed at each other.

"Are you okay?" Sara asked, regretting her question as soon as it left her lips.

Rita sat upright and pointed at her, mascara leaving a dark trail down her flushed cheeks. "Would you be if you'd been told your fiancé was dead?"

"I'm sorry. I had no idea you were engaged. There's no easy way of telling someone a loved one is dead." Sara wondered if her reaction was more about her own guilt rather than losing Joel. A harsh thing to consider, but one that was running through her mind, nonetheless.

"Well, we were, and now I've lost the man I was about to marry in a few months. We were in the process of putting the final details in place for our lavish wedding." She paused and dried her eyes on a coloured tissue she pulled from the box on her desk. "How? How and where did he die?"

Sara inhaled a breath and said, "He was found murdered in his car. I really can't say anything further on that front, not until the pathologist has performed the post-mortem later today."

"Someone killed him? Why? How does that even happen? He was a doctor, for fuck's sake. A man used to saving lives, and here you are, sitting here, telling me that someone has taken his life. How?"

"As I said, I can't go into detail right now. Are you up to answering some questions?"

"About what? No way! You think because I was pissed off with him that I went out and killed him? Are you fucking insane?"

Sara held up a hand. "The thought never even crossed my mind, I assure you. What I would like to know is if Joel has received any form of threat lately, either whilst he was at home with you or during his shift at work."

Rita relaxed into her chair and deliberated the question for several moments. "I don't know. I don't think so. We didn't really discuss his work, too much blood and guts for me to cope with. Yes, he has mentioned that over the last few years patients' intolerance levels were at an all-time low, you know, since the pandemic. Heroes, they were, during that. All back to what it was before Covid struck now, though, people having a go if they have to wait any longer than a couple of hours at A and E. I told him several times to get out of there, to become a GP, or better still, go into private medicine, but he refused to. He said the NHS needed doctors and he was one of the best around. That was my point, he was too good for that place, and now look what's happened, he's dead. Was it a patient?"

"Our suspicion is that it might have been. Although, until we find actual evidence to back up our claim, we can't be sure of that. That's why we're here, to see if Joel had any obvious signs of a physical threat before today."

"I can't think of anything. Are you talking about someone tackling him in the street? Wrecking his car, that sort of thing?"

"Yes, anything along those lines."

She shook her head, and fresh tears welled up. "No. Bloody hell, why am I struggling to get my head around this? He wasn't the type to piss people off, not intentionally. He was the complete opposite, in that he went out of his way to help people. Most doctors are inclined that way, aren't they? Jesus, the money I'm going to lose in deposits now, cancelling all of our wedding plans. No, forget I said that out loud, I appreciate how selfish that must have sounded. That's not me talking, it's the grief. My mind is working overtime, going round in circles because I can't believe he's dead." She covered her face with her hands and sobbed.

"I'm sorry, it's going to take a little while to get used to thinking you're never going to see him again."

Her hands dropped to the desk, and she stared at Sara, her eyes narrowed. "How would you know? Have you ever lost someone that close to you? I mean in the same sort of circumstances?"

Sara's gaze latched on to Rita's, and she nodded. "Yes. So believe me, I do know how you're feeling right now."

"Who did you lose?"

"My husband. He was shot by a gang in Liverpool and he died in my arms."

Rita gasped. "Oh my. But at least you got the chance to say goodbye to him, to tell him how much you loved him, didn't you?"

Tears misted Sara's eyes, and she removed a tissue from her pocket to dab at them. "Yes. It was I suppose what you would call a bittersweet moment."

Rita stared at her, considering her confession, and eventually mumbled, "I'm sorry you had to go through that but I can't help feeling envious of you. At least you were there right at the end."

"I know. I don't think I would have wanted it any other

way. But this conversation isn't about my experience. Is there anything we could do for you? Would you like us to contact a member of your family to come and be with you?"

"No, I have to carry on working, if I don't, well… I dread to think how I'm going to cope. I feel distraught and bereft at the moment, is that natural? How long does the numbness last?"

"I can't answer that. Everyone's grieving process is different."

"All right, how long did your grief last?" she came back to ask.

"Months, may have been even years."

"I couldn't cope with that. How unfair of someone evil to affect my life in this way. Again, I don't wish for that to come across as selfish, but the facts are there, aren't they? The person who killed Joel has not only ruined his life but mine as well. I don't think I'm ever going to be the same, not after this."

"I know it may seem that way right now, but as the saying goes, time is and has always been a great healer. That's what you need to give it, time."

"How can I? We shared everything, and now Joel has been stolen from me." She broke down and cried again.

Carla left the room. She returned holding a glass of water and handed it to Rita who smiled appreciatively.

"Thank you. I'm sorry for breaking down like this. I'm such a hard bitch around here, if the girls see me in this state, I have no idea how they will react to me in the future."

"It's only natural for you to grieve the loss of Joel, I just wish there was more that we could do for you," Sara told her, sincerely meaning every word.

"Life's so unfair, right?" Rita asked with a shrug of her slight shoulders. "What I need you to do is find the person who did this and bang them up for life. No one else should feel the way I am at the moment. Who gives someone the right to take another person's life? To rob them of their last breath? To destroy the happiness they once had?"

"All I can do is assure you that we're going to do our very best to find the culprit." Sara slid one of her business cards across the table. "Here's my number. Put it somewhere safe and don't hesitate to contact me if you need to speak to me at all."

Picking it up, Rita stared at it and twisted it through her fingers. "What happens next? Can I see him?"

Sara resisted the temptation to close her eyes. She had dreaded hearing the question she knew Rita was bound to ask. The last thing she wanted to do was reveal the circumstances behind Joel's death, the fact that if Rita visited his body at the mortuary, she wouldn't be able to recognise him anyway. "I'm going to pass on your details to the pathologist. Once she has performed the post-mortem, she'll be in touch regarding what happens next."

"When is that likely to be?"

"Probably either today or tomorrow, depending on the number of cases to attend to first."

"I see. Will she call me right away? I'm desperate to say farewell to the man I loved."

"I'll make sure she does. We're going to make a move now. I'm sorry we had to meet under such dire circumstances. Ring me if anything comes to mind."

"I will. Thank you for coming and for answering all my questions and for being honest with me about your own experience. I think it has helped me deal with the news."

"I'm glad. I'll be in touch if anything crops up during the investigation."

Sara and Carla said their goodbyes and left the premises.

"Crap, I can understand why you didn't tell her how he died, but all the same, it's going to come as a massive shock to her when she finds out," Carla said on the way back to the car.

"I evaded the truth, I didn't necessarily keep the information from her. I was guilty of putting myself in her shoes, I wouldn't appreciate being told that sort of news. Let his death sink in first, then I'm sure she'll be strong enough to deal with the facts as they stand."

"You think?" Carla sounded unconvinced.

Sara's phone jingled with a text message. Removing it from her pocket, she sighed. "It's from Jane. The conference is being held at two this afternoon. We need to get back to the station, collate all the information we've got on Paul Hanson to date in readiness. I want to hit the public hard and fast with the facts about this bloke."

"You're going to name him?" Carla asked. She entered the car.

Sara waited until she was inside and replied, "Yep. I want his face and name out there. He's obviously still in the area. Joel's death is all the proof we need to recognise that fact."

"What are you going to do about Lorraine? Dare I ask what you intend to do about Ian, the other paramedic, as well? What if Hanson goes after him while we're concentrating on protecting Lorraine?"

"Good call. Okay, you ring the desk sergeant, ask him to send a patrol vehicle over to the hospital. Let's have someone posted outside the entrance at all times until we've caught this bastard."

"On it now. And Lorraine?"

"I heard you the first time. I'm going to chase up DCI Price on that one."

"You think Lorraine is more likely to accept the protection if it comes from higher up the chain?"

"Yep. Or should I say… possibly."

Carla made her call first, and then Sara contacted DCI

Price who confirmed around-the-clock protection had been arranged to cover Lorraine at work and at home. Sara also informed the chief that a press conference had been called at two that afternoon.

"Do you need me to attend?" DCI Price asked.

"Not necessary, ma'am."

"Okay. Give me a shout if you need anything else."

"Umm… has Lorraine been told yet?"

"You want me to do that for you?"

Sara cast a satisfied grin in Carla's direction. "Oh gosh, that would be wonderful, thanks, boss. It's just I have all the preparations to do for the…"

"Yes, yes, Inspector. I'm well aware when I've been cajoled into doing something."

"Me? Never, ma'am, I could never do that to you. You're far too savvy to allow that to happen."

"We'll have words about this later, once we've caught the bastard. Ring me if you need me."

"I will, don't worry."

"I'll get onto Lorraine now. My take is that she'll be on the blower to you as soon as I've ended the call, so you needn't think you've got off lightly."

Sara grimaced and faced Carla who was sniggering behind her hand. Sara jabbed her in the thigh and ended the call.

"Didn't think about that, did you? What are you going to do, ignore her call? I think her line is going to be red hot, matching the colour of her hair."

"Shit, and there was me, rubbing my hands, believing I had got out of it."

"I'd love to be a fly on the wall of your office when the shit starts flying."

Sara growled at her partner, regretting her decision to take the coward's way out.

CHAPTER 9

"What the fuck, Sara? I thought we were friends!"

Sara had run into her office as soon as Lorraine's name flashed on her tiny screen.

"I'm sorry. In my defence, the chief overruled me. She wanted to become involved in the case and took over the responsibility of arranging the protection for you. I did warn her that you wouldn't be happy about it." Sara had her fingers tightly crossed as the white lie tumbled out of her mouth.

"You're not wrong there. As if I need protecting from anyone. You know I'm a black belt in karate and can handle myself if the need ever arose."

"I do. Like I said, the chief was insistent. The last thing I need right now is us falling out about this."

"It was on the cards, but you've managed to talk me down. Anyway, I've got to fly, I'm about to perform the PM on Joel."

"I repeat, are you up to this, Lorraine?"

"For the umpteenth time, that's an affirmative. Stop worrying about me, I'll be fine. He was a dear friend who deserves to be treated well. And no, that's not me having a pop at my colleagues. I would feel the same way if it was your body lying on the slab."

"Christ, that's reassuring. I'll be able to sleep better tonight, knowing that snippet of information."

Lorraine laughed. "You know what I mean. Anyway, where are we with this fucker? Is he still on the run?"

"Yep. I'm getting ready to head downstairs to hold a press conference. We're trying to flush the shithead out into the open."

"Good luck with that one. If there's anything I can do, give me a shout."

"Apart from remaining vigilant at all times, oh, and keeping on top of the lab boys, of course. The more evidence we have against Hanson the better."

"Don't worry, it's all in hand. I've told them to make the case a priority. We do this as a team, Sara, you should know that by now."

"Oh, I do. Hence my being concerned about you. I'm sorry I went behind your back and I'm aware how capable you are of looking after yourself, but we're dealing with an unknown quantity in Hanson. He's a loose cannon because of his mother's death. Hang on, a lot has happened since all this began, I'm not sure if I brought you up to date on this or not."

"On what?"

"You told me that Hanson's mother was poisoned. Well, we brought him in for questioning about it, and he tried to blame the part-time carer. We went to question her, and she flat out denied it then pointed the finger back at Hanson. She presumed he was stitching her up because he caught her in his mother's purse taking some money which his mother had sanctioned. She paid it back the following week, she was in dire straits and Mrs Hanson offered to lend a hand."

"Holy shit! That's one screwed-up fucker we have on the loose if he's trying to pass the buck like that."

"Yeah, which is why—"

"Don't even go there. I'm still pissed off you went behind my back."

"I can't keep apologising, you're just going to have to trust my instincts on this one, okay?"

"All right. We both should be getting back to work."

"Check in with me regularly, if you get the chance."

"Nope, I'm a busy bitch at the best of times. If you want to check in with me then that's a different kettle of fish. See ya."

Sara groaned. She jabbed the End Call button and put her mobile on the desk. She placed her head in her hands. Taking a moment to sort out her thoughts and what lay ahead of her. Pushing aside her friend's anguish for a second or two, Sara jotted down some extra notes for the news conference. A tap on the door, a few minutes later, interrupted her train of thought. Carla didn't wait to be summoned, she dipped her head around the door.

"Is it safe to come in?"

"I wouldn't necessarily say that. What's up?"

"The boys have located something vital on the CCTV footage they need you to take a look at."

Sara flew out of her chair and followed Carla across the incident room to Craig's desk. "What have you found? Make it quick, I need to get going." Her gaze automatically shot up to the clock on the wall. She had five minutes to spare before she needed to be downstairs.

"We finally tracked down the doc's car. It was stuck at the lights here. There was no other traffic in the area. This was around one in the morning. He appeared to be distracted. This guy in the hood entered the passenger side of the vehicle and clobbered him. Then he dragged him into the back seat and drove off."

"Can we get a close-up of the driver on any other cameras in the area?" Sara's heart thumped wildly.

"We're trying now."

"In your opinion, do you think the man could be Paul Hanson?"

"We can run his build et cetera through the software and see what we come up with, but it's going to take time."

"Do it. But, if you had to take a stab at it, would you say the abductor was Paul Hanson?"

Craig and Barry glanced at each other and then at Sara.

"I'd say we were ninety-nine percent positive, boss," Craig said.

"Okay. I'm presuming he drove Joel out to the crime scene where he carried out the deed. What we need to know is how he got back from the location?"

"Could he have driven there during the afternoon, dumped his car and hitched a lift back into the city?" Craig was the first to suggest.

"Possibly. Get the camera footage from that side of town, and I need you to scrutinise every car which entered the city yesterday."

Craig faced her and raised an eyebrow. "That could take days, boss."

Sara shrugged. "It is what it is, Craig. Let's get this fucker nailed down. You guys have done well so far, I'm sure this isn't beyond your capabilities."

"Yes, boss. We'll get to it now."

Sara stepped away from the desk and told Carla to keep an eye on the team while she attended the conference. "I sense we're getting close now."

"I wish I had your optimism," Carla said. "Good luck down there."

"Thanks. All it's going to take is one member of the public

to get in touch, and we could have him sitting in a cell by nightfall."

Carla rolled her eyes.

"Yeah, I know..." Sara said, "you wish you had my optimism. I shouldn't be long."

Sara turned to leave the room, but Carla caught her arm.

"You never said how it went with Lorraine?"

"I'll fill you in when I get back."

"Geez, keep the suspense going, why don't you? Can't you tell me the gist of it?"

"She was fine, sort of."

"That's a relief."

"Yeah, believe me, I'm thanking my lucky stars. See you later."

Sara almost made it to the bottom of the stairs.

"DI Ramsey, hold it right there."

She spun on her heel to see DCI Price charging down the stairs towards her.

"Ma'am, is everything all right?"

"I thought I'd tag along for the ride, so to speak. It's been a while since I attended one of your press conferences."

"Oh, I see, of course. We'll need to get a move on, I'm already running a few minutes late."

"It doesn't do any harm to keep the pack waiting. What about your notes?"

"Shit! I'll be right back." Sara bolted back up the stairs, through the incident room and into her office to retrieve her notebook. She gulped down the remains of her lukewarm coffee and retraced her steps at warp speed.

"Are you all right?" Carla asked.

Sara waved her notebook above her head. "Damn well forgot my notes."

"Oops, not the best start."

Sara caught up with DCI Price and Jane Donaldson in the anteroom.

"You're going to need to take a few breaths to calm down, Sara," Jane warned. "No rush, they'll wait."

"I'm fine, don't worry about me. Are we all set?"

DCI Price winked at her. "That's my girl. We're ready when you are, right, Jane?"

"Absolutely." Jane led the way, followed by Carol Price and then Sara brought up the rear.

Before she entered the conference room, Sara sucked in a few more steadying breaths. Her mouth dried up, and her heart raced when she saw the size of the crowd in front of them. "Damn," she muttered.

"It's not too late, I can take the lead if you don't feel up to it," Carol said.

As tempting as the chief's offer sounded, this was Sara's case, and while she was still standing, she'd see it through to its conclusion.

The journalists behaved themselves for a change, which surprised Sara. Her nerves calmed down relatively quickly after she began the conference, and she found it a breeze compared to some she had held in the past couple of months.

"So, what's his motive?" one of the more eager journalists asked during the Q&A session at the end.

"We won't know that until we have him in custody, and that's not going to happen without the public's help. When a suspect goes to ground, and believe me, we have dozens of men out there searching for Mr Hanson, sometimes it only takes a member of the public to see someone acting strangely, who goes on to report their behaviour, that is often the key to us making an arrest." Sara held up the image they had of Paul Hanson and showed it to the crowd before her. "If you've seen this man, please, please ring the number on the bottom of your screen. I would add a word of caution to this plea as well: the suspect could be armed, he's also extremely dangerous and should not be approached by a member of the public. Call the number and give us the necessary information and let us deal with the suspect. Thank you for your time today."

Sara and DCI Price left Jane to deal with wrapping up the conference and exited the room.

Carol clutched Sara's forearm and smiled. "You did well in there, despite your initial reluctance."

"Thanks. I'm okay most of the time, providing the crowd behave themselves." She held her crossed fingers up. "Hopefully something good will come of it. It won't air until later this evening."

"I take it that you're going to get a member of your team to man the phones."

"Yep, I'll ask for a volunteer. If they've all got plans then I'll stay behind and do it myself."

Carol shook her head. "That's not going to happen, you need your rest to be on top of your game. If none of the team can do it, let me know, and I'll make the necessary arrangements for someone to cover."

"I can do that, boss, there's no need for you to get involved."

Carol raised an eyebrow and tutted. "Too late for that. I want to contribute to this investigation. You're stretched to the max as it is. If this fucker decides to go out on the prowl again tonight, to rob another victim of their life, that's only going to add to the pressure already wrapped around your shoulders."

"I never thought about it like that. Okay, you win. I'll ask Craig to do it, he rarely, if ever, lets me down."

"Good. Let's hope he has a busy night."

. . .

CRAIG AGREED to pulling the extra shift like an eager pup. Sara sat with him, gave him the instructions he needed and even placed an order for pizza to arrive at seven to help combat the boredom which might lay ahead of him, if the response turned out to be lacklustre. She also instructed Craig to keep her updated throughout the evening if anything worthwhile came in from the public.

Then she made her way home for the evening. Stifling a yawn, she rang Lorraine's number. "Hey, just thought I'd check in with you."

"You're too kind. I've told you not to worry about me, I'm more than capable of looking after myself. I have an officer on duty outside my office. I'll be leaving in about an hour, and I'm presuming he's going to be accompanying me home for the evening."

"He will. I'm glad you've backed down and agreed to the protection, love, that's a load off my mind."

"Does he have to stay outside the property all night, or can I invite him in?"

Sara laughed at the sultry tone Lorraine had used. "Behave yourself. If I get a report back from the desk sergeant that you've led the officer astray overnight, there will be trouble, lady."

"Drat, you always spoil my fun. You know it has been a while since I've had a playmate in the bedroom, one worth talking about anyway."

"Oh God, he'd never cope in that case. No, don't you dare, Lorraine Dixon, I need you to show a modicum of restraint. Make him a drink and a sandwich, if you like, but that's all, you hear me?"

"God, who are you, my bloody mother? Yes, Sara, no, Sara, three bags full, Sara."

"Good, as long as you recognise who is in charge, we're

going to get along just fine. Do you need anything before I head home?"

"I don't think so, not unless you want to swap places for the evening?" She lowered her voice and added, "I think Mark tops this guy in the handsome stakes."

"Get away with you, you're a trier, I'll give you that. I mean it, if you need me during the night, ring me. I'm always available to take your calls, Lorraine, remember that."

"And like I've said a million times before, you worry too much. I'll be fine. How did the conference go?"

"It went. Should be airing soon. I've got a member of the team manning the phones for the rest of the evening. He'll call me if there are any major developments."

"Great stuff. Okay, I'd better finish up writing this report for a somewhat impatient inspector we both know and then I'm going to call it a day myself."

Sara chuckled. "You're nuts. I'll check in again before I go to bed."

"I'll look forward to it. Enjoy your evening, Sara, and thank you again for always having my back."

"That's what friends are for. Catch the conference later, if you can."

"Don't worry, already on my evening to-do list. Speak soon, mate, and thanks again, for everything."

Sudden tears blurred Sara's vision. "You're welcome," she managed to squeeze past the lump in her throat. She hung up and wiped her eyes on the sleeve of her jacket then called home. "Hi, I'm on my way. Did we decide what we were having for dinner tonight?"

"Don't worry, I felt like cooking, so it's sorted and in the oven."

"What would I do without you?"

"Starve, no doubt."

Sara giggled. "I think you might be right. I'm ten minutes away."

"I'll be waiting in my usual spot. See you soon."

She hung up with a super-sized smile spreading her lips apart. "I'm so lucky to have you in my life, Mark. So damn lucky," she said aloud.

Mark had nipped home at lunchtime to knock up a beef casserole which he'd put in the slow cooker. It filled the kitchen with a wonderful aroma.

"Crikey, that smells good."

"Let's hope it tastes as good as it smells. How was your day?" He kissed her, removed her jacket and hung it up.

Misty jumped into her arms from the bottom step of the stairs and rubbed herself on Sara's chin.

"What a welcome home. I must be the luckiest girl alive, and, my day was as hectic as usual. I'm still on duty, so you'll have to forgive me if I need to take a call."

"Sounds ominous. Has something else happened today?"

"I'd rather tell you after we've eaten. Oh God, I've conjured up the awful images that I was greeted with first thing this morning."

Mark held up a hand. "Yeah, don't go there, not until after we've eaten. Glass of wine?"

"Please. I'm going to switch the TV on in the kitchen, if that's okay with you? I need to catch the news."

It wasn't something they generally did, normally choosing to have peace and quiet at the dinner table, nothing to distract them from holding a conversation that most families missed out on these days.

"I'll switch it on. Any particular side?"

"I prefer *ITV News*, the BBC presenters always come across as a bit snobby, at least they used to."

"Maybe years ago. I think things have changed a touch now."

He switched channels, and within ten minutes they were tucking into their meal whilst watching the conference on the screen.

"You look good on camera."

Sara rolled her eyes. "Thank you, not that I was fishing for compliments."

Mark cleared the table, and once the conference had finished, they started on the washing up together.

"Are you going to tell me what you've had to contend with today?" he asked.

"Over a glass of wine in the lounge. Can I check in with Craig first?"

"Go for it."

She fetched her phone from her jacket pocket and rang the station. "Hi, Craig. How's it going over there?"

"It's quiet, boss, has been all evening. I watched the conference a few minutes ago, so maybe now it's aired we might be inundated with calls."

"Going by experience, I wouldn't get too excited, not yet. It'll be later on this evening when people decide to call the station, if we're lucky. Have you had your dinner yet?"

"Yes, thanks, boss. It went down a treat."

"Okay, give me a shout if something comes to light."

"I'm making good use of my time, checking through the CCTV footage of the Reynolds' incident."

"Anything there yet?"

"Not so far. It's helping to while away the time, though."

"Good luck."

She ended the call and followed Mark into the lounge. "All quiet with Craig. Sounds like it's going to be one of those nights, poor sod. He's put in a long enough shift today as it is."

"He's young. He'll probably be sat down at his desk texting all of his mates."

"Oh ye of little faith, he's actually making good use of his time and going over the CCTV footage of the latest victim's abduction."

"I hope you find this bastard soon, Sara. Do you have any idea what the murders are about?"

"Not really. We have a rough idea, but it hasn't been confirmed yet. His mother died, and he's been bumping off the people involved in her death. Maybe it's hit him harder than anyone realised."

"Mental health issues aren't really easy to diagnose, are they?"

"True enough. We've put Lorraine under protection. I'll need to ring her later, make sure everything is fine at her end."

"Can I speak openly?"

Sara frowned. "Always. Go on?"

"If she's going to be a target for this guy, then I'm glad she didn't take you up on your offer to stay with us for a few days."

Sara rested her head back against the cushion and sighed. "The thought had crossed my mind. I feel for her. For someone to threaten her, when all she's trying to do is her job, is way out of line to me. She's a tough cookie, but I can tell in her voice that she's struggling nevertheless."

"I suppose losing a dear friend at the hands of this shit is bound to affect her. She'd have to be a callous bitch for it not to."

Sara reached for his hand and kissed the back of it. "Yeah, she's one in a million. I know she kicked up a fuss about the protection but I think she realises it's for the best."

"I bet deep down she's grateful for you going the extra mile for her, I know I would be if I were in her shoes."

. . .

THE REST of the evening flew by until Sara announced that she'd had enough for one day and was ready for bed. She completed her nightly routine and slipped under the quilt but rang Lorraine before she settled down to sleep.

"Last call of the evening, I promise. How are things there?"

"Fine. I told you, you worry too much. It's hammering down outside, so I've told Bobby to come inside tonight, I hope that was okay?"

"It's fine, just tell him to remain alert throughout the night. The last thing we need is him falling into a deep sleep and letting his guard down."

"I'll pass the message along. Goodnight, Sara."

"Sleep well, Lorraine."

Mark joined her, and they shared a brief cuddle before exhaustion swept over her.

CHAPTER 10

The alarm went off the following morning, startling Sara. She had slept deeply and hadn't woken up all night, a rarity for her.

She drifted down the stairs to put the kettle on, let Misty out into the back garden and then trudged back upstairs with two cups of coffee in her hands. She gave Mark his and went into the bathroom, where she jumped back into her daily routine of showering and cleaning her teeth.

Mark smiled as she entered the bedroom wrapped in her bath sheet. "You could stay like that all day, I wouldn't object."

"I think my boss would throw a hissy fit." Sara laughed. She dried her hair, finished the rest of her coffee and riffled through her wardrobe for something different to wear, fed up with going to work clothed in dark suits, but then, if she changed things up now, she figured she'd feel uncomfortable for the rest of the day.

"Why the dilemma?" Mark asked.

She removed yet another outfit and replaced it just as

quickly and then reached for her old faithful, her black trouser suit which she teamed up with a red shirt for a change. "Then, this will have to do. Want some breakfast?"

"I'll come down, I don't have to be in work until nine today, so I might have it in bed."

"Lucky you. I can't remember the last time I had the luxury of eating breakfast in bed."

"Cheeky mare, you had it at the weekend."

She cringed. "Oh yeah, sorry." She ran down the stairs and popped two slices of bread in the toaster and fed Misty while she waited for it to pop up.

Mark snuck up behind her and kissed her neck.

"You smell good," he said.

"Must be the new shower gel. Down, boy, I don't have the time for any extracurricular activity this time in the morning."

"Okay, consider me told."

He decided to eat his breakfast at the table with her. Sara then left the washing up for him to do and got on the road at about eight-thirty. She had almost reached the station when she remembered to call Lorraine to see how she was doing. The phone rang and rang. Sara tried several times and then gave up, deciding that her friend was probably in the shower. She'd try again once she was in her office.

"How are things, any news overnight?" Carla asked, joining her on the way to the main entrance.

"All quiet. I rang Craig a few times and checked in on Lorraine before I turned the light off. Nothing to report."

"I bet Lorraine was in her element with a young man watching over her all night."

"I've tried ringing her, but she's not replying. I'll give her ten minutes or so and try again, just in case she was in the shower."

"Seems likely at this time of the morning. Saying that, doesn't she usually show up for work earlier than us?" Carla queried.

Sara's stomach muscles clenched, and bile rose in her throat. "Don't say that. Shit! I've got a bad feeling about this now."

"Should we go over there and check?"

"Yes. Get in the car." Sara jabbed the button on her key fob, and the doors clunked open. She drove out of the car park, narrowly missing Craig as he entered. She reversed and lowered her window. "We're checking on Lorraine. How did it go last night?"

"All quiet, boss, waste of time being here."

Sara lashed out at the steering wheel. "Damn. Sorry, Craig, I'll make it up to you."

He shook his head. "You don't have to. I'll see you later."

"We shouldn't be long." Sara put her foot down, tempted to hit the siren, but resisted until the traffic was jammed on the outskirts of town. "Sorry, folks, needs must for this lady. Now get out of my way."

"You tell them, Sara. Shall I try and call her?"

"Yes, keep trying." Sara ran through several different possible scenarios during the journey. Each one she dismissed as soon as it cropped up. She refused to consider the consequences. "Try the mortuary as well. She might have forgotten to charge her phone last night."

Carla rang the mortuary, and one of the techs told her he hadn't seen Lorraine since the previous evening.

Sara clicked her thumb and forefinger together. "Okay, get in touch with the desk sergeant, ask him to contact the officer on duty at Lorraine's house."

Carla did just that, and the response left Sara feeling cold all over.

"He hasn't checked in as he was supposed to. Jeff has been trying to contact him for the last fifteen minutes."

"Ask Jeff if he's got any spare patrols in the area. If he has, give them Lorraine's address and tell them to meet us there."

Sara pressed her foot down hard on the accelerator, her breathing erratic as wayward thoughts sprinted through her mind. *Please, please let her be safe.*

The estate loomed up ahead. Sara had already cut the siren and lowered her speed a few roads back. She drew up outside Lorraine's detached house at the same time as the patrol car.

"Glad they've arrived, I haven't got my Taser on me," Sara said. She got out of the car and peered over at the house, searching for any sign of movement in the rooms at the front. Her gaze dropped to the front door. "Shit! Shit! Shit!"

"What's up?" Carla whispered. She followed Sara's gaze and swallowed. "Fuck! We've got to get in there."

"What if…? You're right."

"Everything all right, ma'am?" the taller of the two officers rushed over to them and asked.

"What weapons have you got with you?" Sara asked.

Both men removed their Tasers from their pouches. "Both Taser-trained, ma'am."

"Good. You're aware of the situation?"

"Yes, the local pathologist lives here and one of our colleagues has been guarding her overnight."

The other officer dug the taller one in the ribs. "The door is open."

"Well spotted," Sara replied. "We're unarmed. You're going to need to go in there ahead of us."

The officers didn't need telling twice. They ran ahead of Sara and Carla who hung back and hid behind the privet hedge in front of the house. Sara's mind raced slightly faster than her heart.

Sara strained an ear and overheard one of the officers say to the other, "Shit, Bobby was such a great bloke."

She'd heard enough and ran into the house before Carla had a chance to stop her.

"What the... shit, is he dead? Have you checked for a pulse?" Sara sank to her knees and placed two fingers on the officer's neck. She glanced up at her partner and shook her head. "He's cold, feels like he's been dead for a while." She stood and faced the other officers. "Check the house for Lorraine, start upstairs."

They charged out of the lounge, and the floor thumped overhead, then Sara detected their footfall on the stairs not long after. They appeared in the doorway, both shaking their heads.

"No sign of her, ma'am," one of the men said.

Sara stared at Carla, lost for words. All she could think about was Lorraine, abducted by the killer.

"We'll find her, don't worry," Carla said as if reading her thoughts.

"But will we find her in time? You're forgetting one important fact, he's a serial killer." Sara ran a hand through her hair and tugged at the ends. "He killed his own mother, for fuck's sake. Do you really think he's going to stop when it comes to crunch time?" She looked over her shoulder at the body of Hanson's latest victim. "Ask him?"

Carla shook her head and stamped her foot. "What do we do now?"

"We do anything and everything we can to get Lorraine back before it's too late. Boys, we'd usually visit the next of kin in a case like this, but..."

"Leave it to us to sort out, ma'am," the taller officer said, the colour draining from his cheeks. "We'll have a word with the sarge. He'll want to break the news to Bobby's wife. Shit, she's expecting their first kid, too."

The news only added to Sara's devastation and foul mood.

Carla sensed what was going on in her head and patted her on the arm. "This isn't your fault."

Sara smiled and with tears in her eyes said, "Isn't it? I was the one who let Hanson go."

CHAPTER 11

*L*orraine's head felt like it had been hit by an express train. She sat up in the back of the van, or tried to. It was a struggle with her hands tied behind her back. It didn't take her long to realise she wasn't as agile as she used to be. The more she tried to right herself the more her head throbbed. Her abductor hadn't held back and had wacked her hard, so hard that she thought she might have suffered a fractured skull. She ditched the thought after running her bound hands over her head and finding it intact, however, it still didn't stop her from worrying about the damage he had caused.

She glanced around her. It was all too familiar; he had taken her van. She rarely took it home from work. Why had she chosen to do it last night? It would remain a mystery to her. Lorraine could see the driver up front. She would need to be discreet if she was going to arm herself, just in case the opportunity arose to attack him. To her right lay the evidence bags and to her left the equipment she used to collect any evidence or DNA at a crime scene.

After squirming into a better position, she grappled

behind her, hoping that something sharp would work its way into her hand. Suddenly, the van's movement became rocky, and any thoughts of her finding something of use were overshadowed by her need to remain upright.

Where the fuck are we? More to the point, what are his intentions? I need to find a way to escape him. He's unstable. Why kill the officer who was tasked with protecting me? Why? Bobby seemed such a nice bloke. He had spoken about how much he and his wife were looking forward to welcoming their new addition to the family. They had chosen the colour for the nursery, and he was due to decorate the room at the weekend. Now he's dead and will never lay eyes on the little one. And it's all my fault.

She shook her head to dislodge the memory, but the motion caused her head to hurt even more. Closing her eyes made things a hundred times worse. The movement of the van made her want to vomit. Another couple of knocks and bumps, and the van came to an abrupt stop. She didn't have long. She frantically searched the area behind her, regretting that she was an organised tidy freak. The back door opened as she found what appeared to be a scalpel. She fiddled with the implement and shoved it up her sleeve, at the same time, nicking her wrist.

He grabbed her bound legs and yanked her out. Lorraine thought about screaming but figured, what would be the point? No one would hear her, judging by the ground they had covered on the way to the location.

"Get out here, bitch. Any trouble, and I won't hold back, so get that defiant look out of your frigging eyes, you hear me?"

"You won't get any trouble from me, I promise. Why are you doing this, Mr Hanson?" Mind games; she thought using his name respectfully might go in her favour, maybe even catch him off-guard if an opening surfaced to launch an attack.

He grinned. "You'll find out soon enough. Now let me check you haven't picked up anything you shouldn't have during our little jaunt here."

He spun her around so fast she lost her balance and ended up with her face flattened against one of the back doors.

"I knew it. You women can't be trusted, can you? You're going to suffer for trying to deceive me."

He removed the scalpel and sliced her wrist in the process. "I'm sorry, wouldn't you do the same if you were in my shoes?" Laughing, he threw her over his shoulder, grunting as her weight flopped over his back.

"No, because I would never allow myself to get caught. You and that copper were both amateurish last night. I watched the house for hours before I made my move. He was asleep in the chair when I broke the window in the kitchen to gain access. Dumb shit! Well, he's paid for his incompetence now, hasn't he? With his life." He let out another evil laugh and set off, kicking at the larger stones ahead of him.

Lorraine found it impossible to raise her head to see where they were going as the jerking motion was making her feel sick.

A door opened, and they entered some kind of kitchen, maybe a utility room. He lowered her, not too gently to the floor, and she toppled on the spot for several seconds, the room spinning around her.

"Where are we?"

"Why? You ask a lot of questions. Continue, and each one will come with a punishment."

Lorraine closed her lips tightly, resisting further temptation with that threat hanging over her head. He pushed her in the back, expecting her to walk into the next room, but her ankles were bound too tight, and she struggled to even shuffle, which angered him as he had to give her a fireman's lift once more.

"I'm sorry," she whispered.

"So you should be. You're not exactly stick-thin, are you?"

"I like my food, always have done."

"It's okay, you won't be getting much here, your body will have to call on your reserves to see you through the next few days."

"What are your intentions?" she dared to ask.

He lowered her to the floor and then pushed her into one of the dining chairs by the mahogany table and stamped on her left foot.

Lorraine yelled out. "What was that for?"

"I told you there would be recriminations to any questions you asked."

"I'm sorry. It won't happen again."

He shook his head and sneered, "Who are you kidding, lady? I'll be right back, don't go anywhere." His laughter followed him out of the door.

Lorraine took the opportunity to take in her surroundings. The thick cobwebs decorating the ceiling and the top of the walls suggested that the house hadn't been lived in for a while, and the inch-thick dust on all the surfaces confirmed her suspicions. She peered out of the window and saw a couple of large buildings across a concrete courtyard that made her think this was perhaps a farm, maybe on the outskirts of Hereford. She had no way of knowing how long she'd been unconscious in the back of the van.

Hanson reappeared with a bag and placed it on the table next to her. "Now then, you and I are going to have a blast, well, I'm going to anyway."

"Meaning what?"

He shook his head and tutted. "There you go again, asking

unnecessary questions. Tell me, Dr Dixon, are you right- or left-handed?"

Lorraine frowned and wondered where his question would lead to. "Right."

"And is that the hand that cut my mother open while she was lying on the slab?"

Her eyes closed, and she swallowed, pushing down the acid burning her throat. She wasn't stupid, she had a rough idea what was about to happen next. He rummaged inside the bag and removed a hammer.

Tears blurred her vision as her gaze drifted to the implement she'd had in her kitbag for years, since the day she had started her career.

He hit the head of the hammer against the palm of his hand. "Ah, but first, I'm going to need to untie you." He raised a finger and put it close to her face. "Any funny business, and I'll use that hammer to smash every bone in your body."

"Please, I don't want this. If you injure my hands, I might as well kiss my career goodbye."

He laughed. "That's presuming you're going to get out of here alive."

"What do you want from me? Your mother was already dead before she came my way, you poisoned her."

He bent down and rested his forehead against hers. "Did I? What proof do you have that I was the culprit?"

"The SIO questioned you, and the part-time carer, she told Sara she didn't do it, so this must lay at your door."

"But proof? What proof do you have? No proof whatsoever, not with my mother's death or those of the others I have killed this past week. I was careful. I'm savvy, you see. I watch all these true crime shows on TV, they give us criminals ideas that we would never think of covering on our own."

It had been said many a time before, so Lorraine was

aware of the damage these programmes caused in the long run. Saying that, even the brightest criminal slipped up eventually, as she and her team had discovered over the years.

He untied one of her hands, her right one, and tied the other one to the back of the chair. Lorraine clenched and unclenched her fist to gain the feeling back in her fingers.

He smiled down at her and muttered, "I wouldn't bother. Lay it flat on the table."

Lorraine shook her head. "I won't."

He tapped the hammer against her temple. "Really? That's not the answer I wanted to hear. Do it, or the consequences will be far greater."

Reluctantly, Lorraine placed her hand on the table then snatched it back again. She did this a few times, and each time the hammer tapped against her skull. The final time she put her hand down and left it there and squeezed her eyes shut.

"I'm going to enjoy this." He grabbed her wrist, pinning her hand in place, and whispered, "Eeny, meeny, miny, moe."

"Just do it. Don't make me suffer any more than is necessary, I'm begging you. Do that to my hand, and you might as well stick a dagger in my heart."

"Don't give me ideas, Doctor."

Bang!

Lorraine screamed, her hand ablaze from the strike that had crushed her middle finger. Vomit emerged, and she spat it out on the floor beside her, unable to hold back, which disgusted Hanson.

"That's gross, and you expect me to clean up after you? Think again. I've done my share of cleaning up shit and sick over the past few years. No one knows what we have to contend with as full-time carers. The urge to vomit when you're wiping the shit from someone's arse because they've forgotten how to wipe their own backside. People are deluded if they think caring for someone only consists of sitting with that person day and night, feeding them, washing or showering them. It's the crap in between that people couldn't give a shit about. I hope you never have to contend with the fucking nightmare days I've had to put up with. Caring for an old person is worse than caring for kids. Once the mind goes, that's it. Their capabilities are non-existent. At least kids can figure things out for themselves, but once dementia strikes…"

Lorraine gulped down the sob threatening to come out. "I'm sorry. I didn't realise your mother had dementia as well. I appreciate how difficult it must have been for you."

"Early onset dementia. You're just saying that. No one cares, not when it is happening to someone else."

"Couldn't you have put her in a home?"

"We couldn't afford it. The government saw to that, forcing people to sell up their own properties to pay for a room in one of these blasted homes. I coped all right, in the beginning. Once they saw I was coping, the medical profession couldn't have cared less. I had no support other than that thieving bitch, Tina. I caught her robbing money from my mother's purse one day, saw her in a different light from that day, I can tell you. And yes, she's on my list to punish next, after I've dealt with you. Now where were we? Ah, yes."

He raised the hammer again, and Lorraine screamed even before it struck her hand a second time.

CHAPTER 12

Sara downed her second cup of coffee in quick succession, hoping the caffeine would kick in soon and calm her nerves. Once the news had reached DCI Price, she showed up to lend a hand.

"I'm so sorry, Sara, I know you and Lorraine are close friends. What can I do to help?"

"Thanks, boss. There's little we can do until we bloody find out where he's taken her or… we find her body."

Carol gripped Sara by the shoulders and shook her. "Enough of that. We're not defeatists around here, are we, Sergeant?" she asked Carla, who was standing next to Sara.

"I've told her that already, ma'am. We'll find her. We've got alerts out all over the county now, just in case he decides to leave the area with Lorraine. In my opinion, he'd be foolish to hang around here, knowing that we're likely to pull out all the stops to get her back."

"Any news on the cameras yet?" Carol asked.

"Not yet. The neighbour said he saw a man driving Lorraine's van in the early hours of this morning, at around five, while he was out walking his dog before he left for work," Sara said.

"That's good news. At least we know what vehicle they're in," Carol said.

"Have you got an update for us, Craig?" Carla called across the room.

"I think I've spotted it, Sarge. I'm just making sure it's the right one on a different camera. You know me, I prefer to be thorough."

"Good. Let me have a look at it," Carla said and made her way over to Craig.

Sara perched on the desk behind her and covered her face with her hands. Carol placed an arm around her shoulders. It was a great comfort to Sara, and she appreciated her chief's public show of affection.

"You're going to have to hold it together, Sara, for the team's sake. They're going to be relying on you throughout this ordeal."

Sara dropped her hands and sucked in a steadying breath. "I know. I'm sorry, I'll try. It's just that… after all he's done… killed the other people who had anything to do with his mother's death, it's only natural for me to be concerned about Lorraine and what he's likely to do to her. She was only carrying out her job. This could happen to any of us, if there are warped people like him walking the streets, out for revenge."

"You're thinking too deeply about this, and eventually, it's going to affect your judgement. You need to clear your mind and come up with a suitable plan of how we're going to save Lorraine. I know it's not beyond you, Sara. Give this all you've got, for me."

Sara smiled and nodded. "You're right. Sitting here moping about isn't going to rescue Lorraine, is it?" Sara launched herself off the desk. "What do you suggest we do next?"

Carol raised an eyebrow. "I'm going to pretend I didn't hear you ask that."

"I was joking… I think. I've got this. *We've* got this as a team. Once we track down the van, we'll hit him hard and fast, make him regret the day he ever tangled with us."

"While I admire your enthusiasm, maybe you should tone it down a little, for now."

Sara smiled. "Excuse me while I rally my team."

"I'll sit here quietly and watch a professional at work."

"No pressure there then," Sara replied with another grin. She walked to the front of the room and drew everyone's attention. "In case some of you are unaware, Craig believes he has eyes on Lorraine's van. Once he's confirmed that, I need you all to be prepared to drop everything you're doing and offer him any assistance he needs. I sense we're going to get one chance to grab our friend and colleague, and one chance only. Don't let me down, guys."

"We won't," came the team's response in unison.

It was another fifteen minutes before Craig located the van on another camera. "I've got it. They're heading out of town, on the Worcester Road."

The team pounced, and all set to work, checking possible hideouts along the route. Searching for shortcuts the van might have taken. Frustratingly, there were far too many options open to the criminal along that A-road.

Carol coughed.

Sara spun around to look at her. "Am I missing something?"

"Possibly. Have you considered using the Force's drone?"

Sara's eyes widened. "No, why don't I ever think to use it?"

"With respect, ma'am," Barry called out, "we need to have

a rough idea of which direction the van took first, they tend to home in on a specific area."

The conversation went back and forth for a few minutes until the phone rang, interrupting them all. Jill took the call. She raised her head and immediately caught Sara's attention. Sara shot across the room.

"Sorry, Mr Thomas," Jill said. "I'm going to put you on speaker. Can you explain what you saw to my boss?"

"Hello, yes. I'm a taxi driver. I finished my shift at six this morning. I was driving back from Worcester when this van cut me up. At first, I thought I'd drifted off to sleep behind the wheel but then I realised, no, the van took the corner quickly, and the driver put his foot down going up a road that leads to one of the farms in the area."

"Can you tell us exactly where that is, sir?" Sara asked, her spirits rising by the second.

"It would be better if I showed you. It's one of those turnoffs easily missed if you don't know it's there."

"If you'd be willing to do that for us, that would be great. Do you want us to meet you somewhere en route?"

"Whatever is easiest for you. I should be in bed, but this was pricking at my conscience, and then I remembered one of your lot holding a press conference about a serial killer on the loose and thought I'd better get in touch in case there's a connection. I wouldn't be able to live with myself if there was and I had kept my mouth shut."

"You did right calling us, and yes, we believe there could be a connection. The sooner we can meet up the better." Sara crossed her fingers in the hope that he would agree to meet with her in the next half an hour or so.

"I'm free now, if you like."

"You're wonderful. I can't thank you enough for this. Name the spot, and we'll be there."

"What about out at Whitestone, the new David Wilson estate? I'll park up in the lay-by."

"I know the one. We could be there in fifteen minutes, how does that sound to you?"

"Fine, I'm only up the road, it'll take me five minutes to get there."

"See you there. Sorry, I didn't catch your name?"

"Terry Thomas."

"Great, we're leaving now." Sara handed the phone back to Jill. "Guys, not sure if you got the gist of that or not, but we've got a genuine lead that we need to act upon quickly. Everyone come with me, except you, Jill. I need you to man the phones. Those who are Taser-trained need to collect one on your way out. Everyone else, grab your sprays, cuffs, and anything else you can lay your hands on at short notice and follow me."

"Umm… you're not leaving me behind," Carol shouted from the back.

Sara glanced at Carla who shrugged. "You can ride with us, boss."

THE TEAM LEFT the building en masse. The desk sergeant held the front door open for Sara.

"Have you just got back?" she asked.

"Yes, ma'am. She took it badly, I had to take her to the hospital, they think she might lose the baby."

"Fuck, not what I wanted to hear. Okay, sorry, Jeff, I'll need to deal with that later. We've got a lead as to his where-abouts, we're all on our way out there now." Sara raced ahead to the car.

"If you need any help, ma'am, just give me a shout."

"Send all available cars out to the Whitestone area, we'll let them know what's going on there."

"Consider it done, good luck."

"Thanks, Jeff." Sara jumped in the car with Carla sat beside her and DCI Price in the back at her insistence when Carla had offered to give up her normal seat. "You're going to need to buckle up, boss. I have no intention of sticking to the speed limit."

"I'd be shocked if you did, Inspector. Let's get this bastard."

THEY MET up with the taxi driver in his Mercedes, and together, in a convoy of two unmarked cars accompanied by three patrol cars, they followed Mr Thomas to the top of the lane where the car had cut him up. He pulled over. Sara indicated behind him and jogged up to see him.

"This is it. I hope it doesn't turn out to be a waste of time for you."

"I'm inclined to think positive at times such as this. I can't thank you enough for contacting us. Will you drop by the station in the next few days to give a statement? It'll help when the case gets to court."

"I'll do it later today, once I've grabbed a quick hour or two's kip. I'm on duty again later this evening."

"Again, thanks for getting in touch. Drive safely."

He smiled. "Don't worry about me. I've been driving a cab for over thirty years, I'm one of the safest drivers on the road. That's why it ticked me off the way that moron cut me up. I'm determined to keep my exemplary record until I retire next year."

Sara nodded. "I'd better get going. I have a lot to organise. I don't suppose you happen to know what's up the lane, do you?"

"An old farm. Word on the grapevine is that it belonged to old Jack Sullivan, but he passed away a few months ago. As far as I know, the place has been empty ever since. I think I heard a rumour that it's going up for auction soon. Although, I've been known to get my facts wrong on occasions."

"We'll check it out in force, just in case." Sara trotted back to her car, relayed the information and glanced at Carol in the rear-view mirror. "Are you all right to go in with us or do you want to hang back?"

"No way. I've come this far, I'm not going to turn back now. Go easy. Do you think we should call for armed backup? He's killed, what, four or five people already? Sorry, I've lost count."

"To tell you the truth, so have I, I think it's five, including one of our own," Sara replied.

"That's why he needs to be caught. Now," Carla said.

"We're good to go then."

Carla, radioed the other cars, told them to hang fire.

Sara was the next to speak. "We'll sneak up the lane, view the property from a clearing, if that's possible, and assess the situation from there."

Carla nodded and made the other cars aware of the plan. With the acknowledgement received from their colleagues, Sara drove up the lane, slowly but steadily.

"There." Carla pointed at a gap in the hedge. "It's the farmhouse."

Sara crept up the lane until they came to another gap. "I can't see the van."

"There are barns over to the left, according to Google Earth." Carol handed Sara her phone through the gap between the seats.

"You're right. The van might be stashed away in one of those," Sara agreed.

"What about the drone? We could use that now that we've pinpointed a location," Carla suggested.

"I think it's too late for that. We're here now. It would be better to go in on foot, leave the cars here. It's not like we'll be blocking the road for other residents," Sara said, thinking out loud.

"That's a smart idea," Carol replied.

Sara got out of the car and motioned for the officers in the vehicles behind to join them. "We're going in on foot. I've been told there's only the farm up here anyway. My belief is that we're going to need the element of surprise to tackle this bugger. Let's get closer, and then I'll decide what to do next."

Keeping low, with the hedge shielding their movements, they continued up the lane towards the house. Rounding the bend at the top, Sara held up her hand, ordering everyone to stop. She got down on her haunches and assessed the outbuildings, the ones that could be seen from their position. Then they heard it, Lorraine's terrifying scream, and all Sara's planning was forgotten about.

"We need to get in there, *now*. Who are the Taser users here?"

Four officers raised their hands.

"Come with me. We'll storm the place. Everyone else can join us once we've apprehended the suspect."

"Be careful, Inspector," Carol warned. "I know Lorraine is your friend, but don't take any unnecessary risks that might put her life in jeopardy."

"Don't worry, boss, I won't, but thanks for the reminder."

Sara set off with the four officers, and they made their way towards the farmhouse where she presumed Hanson was holding Lorraine. After her friend had screamed out, an eerie silence had descended, and only an odd chirping of a bird in the distance could be heard. The more steps they took towards the farmhouse, the more Sara's heart thumped. From what she could see there were no windows over-looking their position, so they were able to get closer quickly.

"I need two of you to stay with me." She pointed at the men she wanted to remain with her. "You two go round the back, see if there's a possible way in around there. If you hear another scream, I want you to do all you can to get inside the building."

The men took off, keeping low as before. Sara and the other two Taser-armed officers approached the front door. She tried the handle. It was locked. Sara took a step around the front of the house and spotted a window facing the courtyard. There were two barns over to the right, and she could see the rear end of Lorraine's van parked inside one of them. Not that there was any doubt in her mind that her friend was inside the house.

How do we get in there?

"Can I make a suggestion, ma'am?" one of the slightly older officers said in a hushed voice.

"Of course."

"I think we should go in the back way, there aren't many windows for us to access here."

"I was thinking the same," Sara agreed. "Let's go."

However, before they could move, yet another terrifying scream erupted from inside the house.

"It's too late, we need to get in there, now." Sara tore over to the window and saw Hanson standing over Lorraine with a bloody hammer raised above his head.

Sara banged on the window to gain his attention. Hanson dropped the weapon, shocked by the interruption, and scrabbled on the floor to pick it up. In the meantime, the two officers who had taken up a position around the back, entered the room. Sara stayed where she was but gestured for the other two officers working alongside her to go round the back and join the others.

"Let me in through the front door as well," she called out.

Her gaze was drawn to her dear friend who had spotted

197

her and was crying. Tears slipped down Lorraine's cheeks, making a trail through the blood that had seeped from the nasty wound on the side of her head. The front door opened, and one of the officers let Sara in.

"Drop the weapon. Drop the weapon," the officers repeatedly ordered.

Sara dashed through the front door and into the dining room where Hanson was holding Lorraine captive. It took all of Sara's reserves to remain calm, even though she wanted to attack the bastard for kidnapping and torturing her work associate and friend.

"Give it up, Hanson. There's no way out for you now. Drop the weapon."

Hanson might have dropped the hammer moments earlier, but in his right hand he was clutching a large kitchen knife.

Has he already used that on Lorraine? Was that why she had cried out?

"Why should I? I've got nothing left to live for. They all deserved to die, and I'm going to kill this one, too. I was playing with her, making sure she suffered before meeting her maker, the way she made my mother suffer during her post-mortem."

"She wouldn't have suffered. Your mother was already dead. You saw to that. Her death was down to your actions. You've wrongly punished all those people. Killed them because they tried to save your mother. If she hadn't died of a heart attack, the poison would have got her in the end, and who administered that?"

"Tina did. She tried to kill my mother, I told you."

"Did she? It was all a cover-up for what you were doing to your mother, wasn't it? The years of caring for her had finally taken their toll on you, hadn't they?"

He shook his head, and his hand dipped slightly. With her

Taser drawn, Sara bided her time before she pulled the trigger. He was too close to Lorraine, he could still strike out if he was pushed.

"You have no idea what I've had to put up with over the years. It has been hell."

"I don't doubt that at all, but this was never going to turn out right, was it? No, killing innocent people and kidnapping the pathologist who performed the PM on your mother, how could it? Let her go, Hanson. This was never about you. Lorraine had a duty to perform, to ensure your mother's death was properly reported, that was her right as a human being."

"I didn't mean to do it, she was suffering, we both were. She was no longer my mother, the debilitating diseases, several of them, had seen to that years ago."

Up until now, his gaze had been fixed on Lorraine. Once his head changed direction and Sara knew she had gained his attention, she pulled the trigger. Her patience stretched to the maximum, she didn't have it in her to keep the conversation going with the killer, not when Lorraine was sitting there, bleeding and ultimately suffering.

Hanson's body juddered as the volts ran through him.

"Let go, Sara. Don't do this. I'm fine. Let go," Lorraine's voice broke through the haze that had descended over Sara the minute she had pulled the trigger and Hanson had dropped to the floor.

She released her finger and handed the Taser to the nearest officer while she assisted Lorraine. "What did he do to you?"

Tears of relief tumbled onto Lorraine's cheeks. "I'm fine, a few broken bones that will soon mend. Don't worry about me. Thank you, Sara."

"For what?" Sara asked. She dipped a hand in her pocket to make contact with Carla.

"For coming after me, for not giving up and finding me before it was too late. I'll forever be in your debt."

"Blimey! Does this mean I won't have to wait for days for PM results in the future?" Sara grinned and radioed Carla. "It's me. We've got her. I need you to call for an ambulance."

"Bloody hell. Is she all right?"

"Yes, she's okay. It's safe for you and DCI Price to come in. They're just taking Hanson away."

"Is he still alive?"

"Yes." Sara ended the call and began untying Lorraine's arm from the chair and then moved on to release the bindings wrapped around her ankles. "My hands are shaking too much. Can one of you give me a hand?"

Sara took a step back to allow one of the younger officers access. The wires were removed from Hanson's chest and, appearing dazed, he was hoisted onto his feet.

"Get him out of my sight. Bang him in a cell, I'll deal with him later, once I've made sure my friend is all right."

Hanson glared at Sara and sneered. "Another few minutes, and she'd be lying in one of her fridges down at the mortuary."

Sara ran at him and got up close. "You wouldn't have had the guts. Why didn't you kill her outright, like the others?"

"I told you. She deserved to suffer. She took pleasure in making my mother suffer during the PM. All I was doing was repaying the compliment." He tipped his head back and laughed.

Sara couldn't hold back any longer. She aimed her knee at his groin. Hanson doubled over, and the other officers in the room suppressed their laughter.

"I'll get you for that. Assault by a senior police officer. I've got all of you as witnesses," Hanson cried out. He winced as he was forced to stand upright by the two officers on either side of him.

"We didn't see a thing, mate," the officer on the right said.

"Neither did we," the other officers chipped in.

Carla and DCI Price appeared in the doorway.

"What's going on here?" Price asked.

"She kneed me in the bollocks," Hanson shouted. He gestured towards Sara with his head.

"Good. I would have done the same," Price replied. "Make sure he's secured properly in the back of your car, we wouldn't want this one to wriggle free. He needs to spend the rest of his life behind bars."

The officers removed a struggling Hanson from the room.

"The ambulance is on the way," Carla said. "How are you, Lorraine?"

"I must be honest, I've had better days. Thanks, guys. I knew I could count on you to rescue me, even if you took your time getting here."

Sara laughed and tutted. "There's gratitude for you. Next time you get into bother, I'll make sure someone else is in charge of the case."

"Next time? I'm hoping there won't be a bloody next time. It's going to take me weeks, if not months, to get over this torture session as it is."

Sara squeezed Lorraine's shoulder gently. "What a way to ensure you get cover when you need time off."

They all laughed. A siren wailed in the distance.

Sara handed her car keys to Carla. "I'll accompany Lorraine to the hospital and ring you when I need to be picked up later."

"You don't have to do that," Lorraine objected.

"What about the suspect?" Carol asked.

"I think we should let him stew in his cell for a while," Sara said.

"You might want to do a thorough search on him, he's had access to all my equipment."

Suddenly, they were alerted to a commotion outside. Sara ran through the house and saw the ambulance crew hoisting Hanson out of the car and placing him on the ground. There was blood everywhere. The shocked officers stared at Sara.

"Sorry, ma'am, he must have had a blade down his sock."

It was then that Sara noticed the young officer was holding a hand to his ear. "Did he get you?"

"It's just a nick. I'll be fine."

"Get yourself off to hospital." She approached the paramedics and asked, "What's the prognosis?"

"Not good. He's cut two main arteries. The cuts are quite deep, and his pulse is fading fast."

With that, Hanson's eyes flickered open, and he grinned at her. "Thought you'd got one over on me, did you?"

Sara couldn't hold back. She bent down and whispered, "You're one sick fucker. May you rot in Hell."

"Stand back," the paramedic instructed. "That's no way to speak to an injured member of the public, Inspector."

"I have no regrets. It's the way serial killers should be spoken to. I'm sure his five victims would agree with me, if they were here today."

The paramedic nodded and tried his best to stem the bleeding, but Hanson's eyes stared up at them—he was already dead.

Put out by the paramedic's reprimand, Sara said, "You might want to leave him and see to the pathologist this guy tortured inside, that's who you were called to attend to, after all."

The paramedic seemed suitably embarrassed and contacted base to request a second ambulance to attend the scene. Sara hung around until he'd finished his call and waited for him to apologise before she went back into the house to make the others aware of what had occurred.

"Shit, not what we needed," DCI Price said wearily.

"Not the best outcome, I agree," Sara responded with mixed feelings.

IT TOOK another twenty minutes for the second ambulance to arrive. By then, Sara had dispatched the team and sent Carla and DCI Price on their way.

"How are you holding up?" she asked Lorraine once they were settled in the back of the ambulance.

"I'm okay. I've told you before, you worry too much."

"I'm going to say something else that's going to piss you off as well."

Lorraine frowned. "What's that?"

"I told you that you should have stayed at my place with me. Maybe you'll listen to my advice in the future."

"God, how did I know you were going to say that? And there's little to no chance of me listening to your advice in the future, you know that, right?"

Sara laughed and leaned over to hug her friend. She sat back and grasped Lorraine's uninjured hand. "I'm so glad you're still around to keep me in line."

A lone tear dripped onto Lorraine's bloody cheek. "So am I. I can't help feeling disappointed that the fucker won't have his day in court, though."

"Yep, I'm gutted about that, too. The victims' families will feel robbed they didn't get to see his sentencing."

"I have an inkling they'll be relieved he's dead, I know I am. He was a twisted, mixed-up man. I don't think he would have survived being put in prison."

"He probably would have ended up in a psychiatric hospital instead."

EPILOGUE

*A*t midday, Sara was in full-on panic mode. Mark placed his hands on her shoulders and brought her to a stop in front of him.

"Settle down. Everything is in hand, the meat and potatoes are in the oven, the veg is prepared. You've whipped around with the vacuum and the duster, what's left to do now?"

"Plenty. I need to clean out the litter tray. No one wants to see cat poo in the tray while they're eating, let alone smell the damn thing."

"Yeah, I'll give you that one. I'll do it. They'll be here soon, why don't you have a sneaky glass of wine to calm your nerves?"

"Are you determined to get me drunk? I need to have my wits about me for this meal. Everything needs to be perfect."

"And it will be, now stop worrying."

The doorbell rang, sending her into a frenzy. "Shit, shit, shit, they're early."

"It's probably Lesley. You get the door, and I'll toss the litter tray in the garden, we can sort it out later."

"Good idea." Sara straightened her skirt and pulled her sparkly jumper down over her hips. She then opened the front door to find her sister standing there, a bottle of red in her hand.

"Bugger, I didn't know we were dressing up?" Lesley glanced down at her tatty jeans and old sweatshirt.

"It was Mark's suggestion. Don't worry about it, you look fine," Sara fibbed.

Lesley removed her shoes in the hallway and followed Sara into the kitchen where Mark kissed his sister-in-law on both cheeks and offered her a drink.

"Have you had a busy week?" Lesley asked Sara.

"You could say that."

"I saw you on TV, always a proud moment for me. Have you caught the man you were on the hunt for?"

"Aww... thanks, sis. Yes, we arrested him, but he killed himself before we had a chance to interview him."

"Bloody hell. He managed to kill himself in his cell, did he?"

"Nope, en route to the station, kind of."

Sara ran through the details of the arrest, and Lesley seemed suitably shocked by how the events had unfolded.

"You're amazing, Sara. I don't know how you manage to catch all these dangerous criminals."

"I'd say it was all in a day's work but I'd be lying. I have an exceptional team behind me. The stakes were raised when the killer abducted one of our own. Even DCI Price was desperate to get a piece of the action."

"Heck, doesn't that stifle your abilities, having your senior officer there with you?"

"Not really. As DCIs go, she's pretty easy-going. How has your week been?"

"Boring, as usual. Maybe I need to look at changing my

career at some point, I never have anything exciting to tell you when I visit. The dinner smells delicious by the way."

"We're not in competition to see who has the most exciting job, you know. And the dinner is down to Mark, as usual."

"I wish I could meet a man like you, Mark. All the men I seem to latch on to turn out to want another mother to look after them."

The doorbell rang, and Lesley frowned. "Oh heck, now I'm nervous."

Sara smiled. "Don't be. They don't know you're here. I'll be right back."

"GREAT," her sister muttered as Sara left the kitchen.

She opened the front door and smiled broadly. "How are you both?"

"All tickety-boo with us, love. My daughter, the regular heroine." Her father leaned in for a hug and kissed her on both cheeks.

"Stop embarrassing me."

Margaret entered the house first, and her father took her coat from her and hung it up on the rack. Then they both removed their shoes, and Sara led the way back into the kitchen.

Opening the door she shouted, "Surprise! Lesley has decided to join us."

Lesley spun around and spilt a drop of wine on the tiled floor. She cursed under her breath, and Mark mopped it up with a piece of kitchen towel.

"Dad, Margaret. How lovely to see you both. I hope you don't mind me gate-crashing your Sunday dinner?" The colour rose in her sister's cheeks as her father and then

Margaret stepped forward to kiss her. "Forgive me for not dressing up, not sure what I was thinking."

"It's a pleasure seeing you again, Lesley, it's been far too long, and no apology is needed, you look just fine to me," Margaret said. She tucked her arm through Lesley's and guided her to the table. "You sit next to me, dear, we'll have a little catch-up of our own while the others finish off the dinner."

Lesley's face was a picture, and Sara turned away before her sister could see her snigger.

"Don't be wicked," Mark whispered in her ear and draped an arm around her shoulder.

Her father watched on warily, but after a few minutes, his shoulders relaxed, and Mark handed him a drink.

"Everything is going to be fine, Dad. She's told me she wants to make amends. Keeping her at a distance appears to have done the trick. She's finally realised what she's missing out on. How lovely of Margaret to be so forgiving, in the circumstances," Sara whispered in his ear.

Her father smiled. "That's the type of woman she is. I'm surrounded by strong, independent, but caring females and, let me tell you, I wouldn't have it any other way."

"She's a wonderful lady, and you deserve another dose of happiness, Dad." She turned to Mark and said, "We all do."

Her father kissed her forehead and clinked his glass against hers. "We do indeed. I have the best daughters a man could ever want."

THE END

THANK you for reading Son of the Dead, Sara and Carla's next adventure can be found here **Evil Intent.**

Have you read any of my fast paced other crime thrillers yet? Why not try the first book in the award-winning Justice series Cruel Justice here.

OR THE FIRST book in the spin-off Justice Again series, Gone In Seconds.

WHY NOT TRY the first book in the DI Sam Cobbs series, set in the beautiful Lake District, To Die For.

PERHAPS YOU'D PREFER to try one of my other police procedural series, the DI Kayli Bright series which begins with The Missing Children.

OR MAYBE YOU'D enjoy the DI Sally Parker series set in Norfolk, Wrong Place.

OR MY GRITTY police procedural starring DI Nelson set in Manchester, Torn Apart.

OR MAYBE YOU'D like to try one of my successful psychological thrillers She's Gone, I KNOW THE TRUTH or Shattered Lives.

KEEP IN TOUCH WITH M A COMLEY

Pick up a FREE novella by signing up to my newsletter today.
https://BookHip.com/WBRTGW

BookBub
www.bookbub.com/authors/m-a-comley

Blog

http://melcomley.blogspot.com

Why not join my special Facebook group to take part in monthly giveaways.

Readers' Group

Printed in Great Britain
by Amazon

41639991R00126